The Storm Without

Tony Black lives in the west coast of Scotland. An award-winning journalist, he is the author of some of the most critically-acclaimed Scottish crime novels of recent years. *Paying for It*, was followed by *Gutted, Loss, Long Time Dead, Truth Lies Bleeding* and *Murder Mile*. Find out more about the author at www.tonyblack.net

Praise for TONY BLACK

'Tony Black is my favourite British crime writer.'
Irvine Welsh, author of *Trainspotting*

'Tony Black is one of those excellent perpetrators of Scottish noir ... a compelling and convincing portrayer of raw emotions in a vicious milieu.'
The Times

'If you're a fan of Ian Rankin, Denise Mina and Irvine Welsh this is most certainly one for you.'
The Scotsman

'Black renders his nicotine-stained domain in a hardboiled slang that fizzles with vicious verisimilitude.'
The Guardian

'Ripping, gutsy prose and a witty wreck of a protagonist makes this another exceptionally compelling, bright and even original thriller.'
The Mirror

'This up-and-coming crime writer isn't portraying the Edinburgh in the Visit Scotland tourism ads.'
The Sun

'Comparisons with Rebus will be obvious. But that would be too easy ... Black has put his defiant, kick-ass stamp on his leading man, creating a character that deftly carries the story through every razor-sharp twist

Record

'Wonderfully written, tough, edgy, and very dark, but with the odd flash of humour. Tony Black is a brilliant writer.'

Big Beat from Badsville

'Powerful, focused, and intense ... and then it gets better. Get your money down early on this young man – he's dead serious and deadly accurate.'

Andrew Vachss, author of *Hard Candy*

'Tony Black is the Tom Waits of Crime fiction, yes, that good.'

Ken Bruen, author of *London Boulevard*

'Tony Black is already one of my favourite living crime writers.'

Nick Stone, author of *Mr Clarinet*

'This is pure noir, sublime and dark as a double dram of Loch Dhu.'

Craig McDonald, author of *Head Games*

'If you haven't read Black, you're missing out on one of the best new voices to emerge from Scotland in the last few years. One of the best new voices to enter the genre, period.'

Russel D. McLean, author of *The Lost Sister*

'Black is the new noir.'

Allan Guthrie, author of *Two-Way Split*

For Cheryl

THE STORM WITHOUT

TONY BLACK

Published by McNidder & Grace
4 Chapel Lane, Alnwick, NE66 1XT

First Published 2012

©Tony Black

A catalogue record for this work is available from the British Library.

ISBN: 978-0-85716-040-9

Designed by Obsidian Design

Printed by Short Run Press Ltd, Exeter, UK

Cover photo by Euan McCall. Model: Chris Taylor.

Acknowledgements

The Storm Without had been worrying the latches of my imagination for a few years before Cheryl McEvoy of the *Ayrshire Post* gave my idea the green light in the form of a serialisation. I had just moved back to my old home town of Ayr, I'd been away for quite a few years, and wanted to draw on the experience. The thought that Doug Michie would similarly rock back to Auld Ayr and find himself immediately immersed in bother appealed to Cheryl and without her the book might never have been written. So, big thanks to Oor Chez for that, and for making the serialisation such a success.

There's a host of other people I'd like to thank, and probably even more that I will leave out unintentionally, so in no particular order: Chris Taylor for playing Doug in the *Post*'s 30-odd week serialisation. I dread to think what turning up and looking that gloomy did to you Chris, but thanks, mate. And, also photographer Euan McCall – who did such a great job on the film-noir look, week after week. And, Lucas Barraud at Su Casa, thanks for keeping the coffee supplied.

To the folks I re-connected with whilst in Auld Ayr, I'd also like to say a huge thank-you for rekindling old (and very useful) memories: Jim Murray, David Wilson, Mark Stellard, Phillip Smeeton, Fraser MacIntyre, Lorna Munro, Nicola Brown, Jakki Ross and Bob Daliwal in particular.

And as always, thanks to my wife Cheryl for just about everything.

The storm without might rare and rustle,
Tam did na mind the storm a whistle.

Tam O'Shanter
by
Robert Burns

Chapter 1

I knew the place – or should that be *had* known. Auld Ayr Toun had changed. But hadn't we all? I couldn't say I'd weathered any better – though I'd likely seen as many storms in the two turbulent decades since I'd left the town where I grew up, and perhaps knew better than anywhere else in the world.

I watched the wind batter the once-familiar coast, charge the brae as Ailsa Craig sat granite-firm, blanketed in the sea's blackness. I put up the car window and engaged the clutch. The engine purred, spluttered a little on the gear change. I still hadn't adjusted to the TT's biting point. The Audi, likely, had too much poke for me; I was more used to the hammered Mondeos we used in the force.

I shouldn't say 'we' – I wasn't part of the constabulary anymore. Had I moved on, or simply been moved out? I hadn't found an answer to that yet, but I knew Belfast and the RUC was behind me now.

I planted the foot, took a wind of road close in to the gable of a dry-stone dyke. My mind raced into reverse as the twisting coast and glimpses of white sands stretched out before me. I was heading home, to Ayr. To names and places I knew. To Wallace Tower. To Burns Statue Square. To Cromwell's Citadel. The town had a history, much farther reaching than my own, but there was some of it we shared. Those years of my boyhood, my schooling, and the few early years of adulthood when I decided there was more to see beyond the limitations and bournes I'd grown so used to.

So, I'd moved away. But had I moved on?

Someone once said, *experience is the name a man gives to his mistakes*. I knew I had more than my fair share of experience. And much of it had been mistakes. The wife. The drink. The job. Always the job.

I could still see the day I left home for the force's training at Tulliallan; I'd been cocky, full of the arrogance of youth. Ayr was too small for me; it was for people like my parents. The place had nothing to offer me, or so I thought, then.

I had rated my parents as idiots for spending their lives in the same, small place; but now I wondered if I wasn't the idiot. The question had haunted me lately, along with many others: I was questioning everything. Was it my time of life? I didn't know. That was the problem. I didn't know much; my life had become a blank page to me. I was going to have to go back to my roots to make any sense of the mess I'd made of everything since I lost the last thing I had: my profession.

'The Troubles are over, Doug,' the Chief Super had told me. 'At least, they are for you anyway.'

'What's that supposed to mean?'

He'd smiled. A wry one. 'I don't think you need to ask.'

He was right. It had been an instinctual remark; months of living on my nerves, and Irish coffee, had dulled my senses and sharpened my tongue.

'Isn't there supposed to be a ceremonial handing over of a cardboard box … an invitation to clear my desk?'

He rose, turned his back on me as he stared out of the large window that overlooked the station car park and the back of the canteen where kitchen staff sat smoking and gossiping in the sharp Belfast air. 'You don't have a desk ... Not here, not anymore.'

I felt my blood surge, and a strong urge to rabbit-punch the back of his head. I wanted to smash his smarmy grin into the window, but I found a line of cool, looking back, from God knows where.

'Well, that doesn't bother me so much,' I said. 'You see, there are some of us that are a little too attached to our desks, but I'm not one of them, Chief.'

He turned, bit. 'Wisecracks to the end, Doug, eh?' His eyes flared. I'd got to him. He couldn't hide it. His type never could. 'Will you ever learn?'

I let a second or two of stilled silence stretch between us, then, 'Maybe ... maybe.' I pressed out a grin. 'I'll have some time to catch the odd Open University slot now, so you never know.'

He shook his head, made his meaty neck quiver, then crossed the carpet towards his desk. The room around us felt electrified with tension. This was new territory for both of us, and neither of us wanted a return to the old. 'You can live well on an officer's pension, Doug. Just make sure you live quietly.'

'*Or?*'

He let his top lip curl down the side of his face, spoke softly. 'Or you won't live at all.' A full smile erupted. 'Jesus, Doug, you don't need me to tell you how this town works ...'

Belfast wasn't home anymore.

But Ayr hadn't been my home for a long time either. It had been, once. I remembered: my school days reciting Robert Burns at Ayr Academy, my late teenage years partying at the Bobby Jones; but the race to adulthood and the desire to spread my wings had taken me far from those days.

As I neared the Auld Toun I felt a tightness in my chest. I had been back before, back to see my ailing mother; but they were short stops, passing through. Never more than a week. This was different. This was a *sort of* homecoming; the thought gored me.

I dropped the revs on the Audi, eased past the first few houses that had stretched into what I still knew to be Doonfoot. I'd gone north from the airport to collect the car; it had been an impulse buy, a shiny, almost new sports coupé that promised to drive me far away from my troubled past.

I wanted a fresh start, but I was too old for that. I needed familiarity too; and my mother needed me. As I reached the tip of Alloway, the edge of Belleisle, I felt a strange constricting in my guts. Not quite panic, not unease exactly either, but an almost supernatural feeling that I was driving towards old demons, to past hurts, and to more grief. I'd no idea where this came from; there was no reason for it. But I couldn't deny it either. I was still a cop inside, and I lived on those instincts; my life had depended on them, more than once.

The tensed stock of energy in my arms made my wrists ache. I loosened my grip on the wheel, took the window down a few inches and manoeuvred my face towards the cool breeze. My eyes smarted as the air whipped through the narrow gap in piercing jets, but immediately focus returned, my jaw clamped tight in a vice of shock.

'Holy ...'

I knew the face; it hadn't changed in nearly twenty years.

I let my foot rise from the accelerator, pressed in the brake. The TT slowed to a near stop as I edged closer to the bus shelter. She was weighed down. As I drew nearer, I saw her 'brows sat furrowed above tired eyes. Something played behind the eyes though, a sharp intelligence tempered with a cruel anxiety. I'd seen the look a million times before. It was the look worried mothers brought with them to the station after calls in the wee hours about wayward sons and damaged daughters.

I flicked on the blinkers as I brought the car to a stop. Some rain evacuated from a divot in the tarred road surface beneath the car. I sat staring for a second, toyed with my opener – somehow, it didn't seem right to shout through the window. I eased out the door and stepped onto the road. As I walked towards the bus shelter I watched the solitary figure standing there playing with the strap of her shoulder bag. For a moment, time seemed to alter slightly; the air became thick, muggy. She turned, her already large brown eyes widening as she took me in. A narrow aperture appeared in her lips in an attempt to speak, but no words came from her.

I crossed the few steps from road to kerb; my heartbeat ramped as I reached the woman. My steps felt heavy on the damp pavement; my knees loosened a little. A mash of old memories flooded in, some good, some bad. Past times, when we were both different people.

I watched her turn a stray tendril of dark hair behind her ear as she stared at me.

'Lyn …'

Chapter 2

The woman before me looked back, seemed to let a pause enter her thoughts, then turned away. I guess it was what you'd call a *moment*. The last time I had seen Lyn she was another world away. A lifetime ago. I'd met her at Ayr Academy, how or when I couldn't place. She was one of the myriad faces that sat in science class. A girl in a blazer. Long legs on the hockey pitch. A smoker from round the corner at Dansarena. I allowed myself an inward laugh; we were snoutcasts before the smoking ban even existed.

The wind bit, blew a gale down Racecourse Road. I pinched the lapels of my jacket together, felt a shudder pass through me from the wet ground below. My steps fell slowly, soft splashes underfoot. I had a strange feeling turning inside me, a self-consciousness; I was wary in the open. This was Ayr, my old home town: who else was going to appear? Did I want to be recognised? Did I want to reconnect? As I eyed Lyn, hunched on the ledge that passed for a seat in the bus shelter, I knew at least I wanted to reconnect with her. I say *want*, the feeling was more of a compulsion than anything else – I was drawn to her.

At every low point in my life, there was one common denominator. Beyond the despairs, the hurts, and the let-downs was the wisdom of our national poet, Burns.

Rabbie had been there when my marriage finally ended, reminding me of my stupidity with those lines from Tam O'Shanter implanted in my youth:

Ah, gentle dames it gars me greet, to think how mony counsels sweet. How mony lengthened, sage advices, the husband frae the wife despises

I remember returning to an empty, wifeless home. There was a car sitting outside. I tensed, the old alarm bells ringing. The Glock pistol I kept in the glove box came out; I dropped the revs and swept past the parked car with a damp finger on the trigger. My heart rate ramped, then dropped when I spotted Old Tommy sitting behind the wheel of the parked Cavalier.

'What are you doing here?' I said, braking hard.

He wound down the window, leaned out a little. 'I thought you could do with a friend.'

He'd never been more right. And Tommy was always right. Had always kept me right.

We trashed a bottle of Bushmills, and whatever else I had in the house. I don't know what we spoke about; football maybe, the price of bread. It didn't matter. Blokes don't do personal. We do distraction. So when Tommy hit me with a blast of wisdom on his way home it near winded me. He said, 'Doug, she was only passing through ... '

'You what?'

'Angela ...'

The way he said my ex-wife's name, the jolt it put in my heart, made me feel like I'd never heard the word before.

He went on, 'Some people, mate, they're only in your life for a limited time. They pass through, they teach you something, maybe you teach them something too. When the lessons are over, they leave.'

I looked at him, sad Irish eyes intoning me to pull myself out of the spiral I was tangled up in. 'And are you passing through, Tommy?'

He smiled, leaned forward and planted the broad heel of his hand on my shoulder. 'Some of us stick around ... you can't get rid of me so easy.'

I closed the door on him and went back to the bottle.

I knew I was drawing on all kinds of past memories now; it could have been my age. It could have been part of the healing process. A new mindset maybe, the onset of melancholia. There was very little I knew about myself now; maybe that's why I was reaching for the past, for familiarity.

In the final steps towards the bus shelter the rain kicked up, came down in heavy stair-rods that leapt a foot-and-a-half off the pavement. I jogged over the flags towards cover. Under the shelter the rain pounded a rough percussion on the roof. I watched the lonely figure before me; she fingered at the hem of her coat. I started to wipe my shoulders dry, moved forward. As I stood beside her, I was crouched over slightly, my head tipped to the side.

She turned, 'Oh ...'

I stepped back. I'd startled her. 'Sorry ...'

I took a step away; I was in her space, it seemed.

A headshake, 'It's okay.'

I raised a palm, directed it towards her. 'It's Lyn, isn't it?'

I knew she recognised me too, but for reasons of her own she was playing coy. Squinting her eyes and tightening her jaw. Pretending to search her memory banks for the label on my photograph. Closer now, I could pinpoint miniscule changes I'd missed from the car. Her hair was darker than I remembered, probably dyed. Laughter lines sat in faint rows at the corner of her eyes. She smiled less; she smiled a lot less.

'Doug ... Doug Michie. God, it must be I don't know how many years.'

'Too many probably.'

9

Now a smile. 'Best not to count, you mean?'

'Too right!'

We chatted, found some common ground. Old ground. She seemed to be, if not chilling, relaxing slightly. I watched odd glimpses of the girl I'd known come and go. But the heavy air of despair that seemed to surround her clung, never left her. It was as if any burst of laughter, a brief smile even, had to be shut down quickly. She was never far from whatever it was that burdened her. She wore it like a pall.

'Look, I don't see much sign of a bus. Can I give you a run anywhere?' I said.

'Well, where are you going?'

I hadn't given that much thought. 'The town, I guess ...'

'Are you staying?'

I shrugged. 'Yeah, for a time.'

'Well, where?'

I hadn't given that much thought either. 'We'll see.'

She thinned her eyes, turned her neat chin towards her shoulder and frowned over the bridge of her nose. 'Doug Michie ... you haven't changed!'

'Let's get out the rain anyway, warmed up ... how about I shout you a coffee?'

She looked unsure, gripped the strap of her bag and held her hand there. I was confident a rejection followed, but she surprised me: 'Okay. I know a place.'

Lyn sheltered under her bag as we ran through the rain towards the car. My breath was still heavy when we got inside; the windows steamed. I turned on the heater, cleared the windscreen and pulled out. I stared towards the rain-pelted old racecourse and had a smile to myself.

'I remember playing footy out there ... in weather like that.'

Lyn leaned her head forward, eyed the grey sky. 'No-one playing today though.'

'They wouldn't let kids play in that these days ... there'd be a court case.'

Lyn's face changed, grew darker than the sky above. I felt my throat constrict; an urge to correct myself appeared, but I didn't know what I had said to upset her. I tried to lock it down, stared front. I planted the foot to beat the lights. At Wellington Square the rain was bucketing down. I hit the roundabout, took the exit after the Sandgate, and followed the road round the bus station.

I wanted to speak now, say something, anything. But I couldn't find the words. I watched Lyn's pained expression as she stared out the window and felt grateful for the noise of the heater – I wondered if it had stopped the atmosphere inside the car from freezing over completely.

'The coffee shop's round there, past the club.'

'In the wee arcade?'

'Aye, the Lorne Arcade.'

I nodded. The name of the place registered at once – I felt myself settling back into Auld Ayr, if not settling over what I'd said to upset Lyn.

'I'll park at the old Tesco.'

She smiled. 'The old Tesco? ... Haven't heard it called that for donkey's.'

I was glad for the ice-breaker, smiled back. 'I could tell you a story about that joint – nearly cost me my place in the force.'

'Really?'

'Yeah, it was one of my schoolboy pranks. Shoplifting a pack of Tunnock's caramel wafers and a bottle of ginger!'

She ventured a little laugh. 'And you got caught, I take it?'

'Oh aye. Marched into the manager's office and made to stare at my shoes for half an hour while he threatened to call my parents.' I was grinning at the memory. 'Think it was then I decided I wasn't cut out for a life of crime.'

I collected my ticket for the car park, spotted a space and parked up. Lyn seemed to have returned to silence once more. I prattled on. 'Aye, I was lucky the manager didn't call in the police, might have put me off joining up. Contact with uniform is never a good thing for boys that age, unsettles them.'

Tears suddenly burst from Lyn. She lunged forward, dropping her head in her hands.

'*Lyn* ...'

Her shoulders shook as she wailed in hurt.

'Lyn ... what is it?' I felt lost, saddened for her. But confused. I knew she was weighed down, worried, though I'd no clue what about. She seemed broken.

I placed a hand on her trembling frame, 'What's the matter?'

She turned round; her eyes were lined with red, her cheeks now streamed with rivers of black mascara. I watched her mouth twist into a rictus as she struggled for a jumble of words. 'It's Glenn ... they've taken him.'

Something stirred in me, an old instinct. A bit of police training perhaps. I turned in my seat to face her. 'Who's Glenn?'

She spluttered, 'My boy ... my son.'

She buried her face in her hands once more and rocked to and fro. Her tears were choking her as she tried to grasp for breath.

I took her hands in mine, motioned her to straighten herself and take some air. She was hysterical, stripped of all dignity.

'Lyn, look at me.'

She turned.

I lowered my tone. 'Now tell me, who has taken your son?'

Her lips started to quiver as she tried to speak.

Chapter 3

The coffee couldn't come quickly enough. I sat with my back to the counter, turning every few moments to check the waiter's progress at the machine. I was glad to be out of the rain, indoors. When I had last been in Ayr, coffee came in a mug, was instant, and strong. The taste made you wince, near stripped the enamel off your teeth. Now even the Auld Toun had become part of the coffee revolution; it was a welcome change, but right now, the process was taking too long.

In front of me, my former school friend sat meddling with the corner of a cardboard menu. I smiled at her, tried to insinuate some sense of normality into the proceedings but I knew what she was about to reveal would be a heartscald. Likely, to both of us. I wondered if I was really the person for her to be unburdening herself to; I had enough troubles of my own to contend with. Something told me she needed help though, and I'd always been a sucker for a friend in need.

I leaned back in my chair, eyed the soft furnishings and chi-chi décor. 'Nice place.'

Lyn's eyes brightened; she looked around her. 'Yeah, good coffee too.'

I smiled. 'It's a step up on the old greasy spoons I remember about the town.'

'Oh, they're still there … you just have to know where to look for them.'

Lyn dropped the menu. I drummed a finger on the surface. 'No roll 'n' slice?'

Almost a laugh. 'No there is not! … I bet you're still a pie and beans man.'

'You cannae beat a good cow-brain pie, Lyn.'

We were laughing now, both thawed.

Our coffees arrived.

'You not want a caramel log with that?' said Lyn.

'I was always a wafers man.'

The smiling continued and Lyn's face lost its tense angularity, became familiar once more. She seemed to shed the years; a look in her eyes took me back years anyway. I recalled her as she was when we were at Ayr Academy: she had always been headstrong, sure of herself. If I had to pick anyone from our circle to have made something of themselves, move onward and upward, it would have been her. It didn't seem right to see her sitting before me, bruised by a lifetime of domestic defeats. Another victim of the long and winding road we all have to travel towards that certain end. Someone once said: the world breaks us all, and makes some of us strong where the breaks are. Lyn was not one of them. She wore her breaks like battle scars.

'So, you were going to tell me something …' I let the words hang between us like dead air.

She sipped her latte, lowered the cup towards the saucer. A twitch played on her eyelid and she wiped it away with her fingertips. 'The empire biscuits look nice.'

I touched her sleeve. 'Lyn, that's not what we came here to talk about.'

'I know. I know.'

'If you've changed your mind, that's fine too …' She was not the type of person used to unburdening herself on others; she was shouldering too much on her own. I felt pushed to help but wondered if I wasn't interfering, if it would be better for both of us if I backed off; but that wasn't my style. 'I think you want to talk, though, and I'll listen.'

She nodded.

For a moment there was a hush in the coffee shop, then the door whooshed open and a red-faced man in a beanie hat walked in. He made a joke with the waiter about selling flippers for the road out, but few in the place registered more than a forced smile in response.

I turned my gaze back to Lyn.

She spoke, 'When I saw you, out at the Old Racecourse, I'd been walking from the town.'

'In this weather ...'

She sucked in her lower lip. 'I'd been at the court.'

'That's a fair trek, from Wellington Square.'

'I just came out of the court and walked along the front for a bit, along the Low Green, and before I knew it ...'

I picked up my coffee cup, raised the brim to my lips. It was still warm; it was very good coffee. 'Can I ask, why were you at court?'

Lyn scrunched up her eyes; tight radial lines speared into her features. Her nose turned up a little as she tried to speak. 'Glenn ... he was ...' She stopped herself, reached into her bag and removed a small packet of paper tissues.

'Take your time,' I said.

She struggled to get the packet open, ripped into it with her long fingernails, then patted at the edge of her eye with a white tissue. I watched her for a moment as she regained her composure, spoke again. 'A few days ago, Glenn appeared at my door.'

'He doesn't live with you?'

'No. He has a flat down at the harbour ... it was one my ex gave me, when he left.'

15

'Go on ...'

She scrunched the tissue in her hand. 'He'd had a row with Kirsty.'

'*Kirsty?*'

'His girlfriend. They both lived in the flat. I wasn't sure about it at first. They were only eighteen but it was what they wanted and ...'

'I understand.'

Lyn looked out the window, drew a deep breath. 'When Glenn showed up he said it was over between them, they'd had some spat, but they'd had them before so I never thought anything of it, until ...'

I took another belt on the coffee, gave her time to focus her thoughts.

She continued, 'Until the police showed up the next day and told me that they wanted to take Glenn in for questioning.'

'Why did they want to question your son?'

She dropped her gaze, removed the tissue again. 'Kirsty ... they found her in the flat, she'd had some kind of fit. She was epileptic, but hadn't had a fit for years and years ...'

'*Was?*'

Tears came again, slow at first and then more steady. Lyn tried to avoid staring at me; it was as if she couldn't bring herself to utter the words. 'Kirsty's dead ...' She bit her lip for a moment. 'Doug, they think my son killed her.'

I took Lyn's hand in mine. 'Look, they won't have made an allegation like that without some kind of evidence. What did they tell you?'

I could feel Lyn's hand, cold and trembling within mine. Her words trickled out, 'There was bruising on her neck. They think there was a fight and that she fell into a fit and choked on her tongue ... God, Doug, they blame him. They blame my boy.'

I removed my hand, rubbed at her arm. 'Okay. Okay. Let's try and keep it together, Lyn. You'll be no use to Glenn if you fall apart. Do you hear me?'

'Yes.'

'Good. That's good. Now tell me, what happened at the court?'

She flustered, her eyelashes batting quickly as she spoke. 'Erm, they took him.'

'So he's been remanded in custody.'

'Yes, they set a trial date ... one month or so away.'

I felt my head shaking involuntarily. 'And what was the charge, can you tell me?'

'Of course ... they charged him with murder.'

Chapter 4

The boy was on a murder charge. Did it get any more serious?

I knew the answer to that question, but shoved it to the back of my mind. If there was one thing I didn't need right now, after all I'd been through, it was getting involved in another murder. There was a bolt twisting in my stomach that told me Lyn had every reason to be doubtful that her son was involved, but the facts remained.

Someone had been murdered.

Police don't mess about with charges like that. Even the worst kind of plod – the sodden-earth country brigade – knew better.

I rolled the thought over in my mind. Glenn was in the mincer, no doubt about it. A pretty young girl had been killed. No matter who the real culprit was, that was a story that stuck. The boy would carry those allegations for the rest of his days.

I knew Ayr. I knew small Scottish towns. There was a brutal crowd in these places, a sub-section of society that liked to see people hung out to dry. The Ochiltree author George Douglas Brown knew it as well – but I didn't need to re-read *The House with the Green Shutters* to have that confirmed.

I turned the key in the ignition; the TT purred to life. I pulled out, headed for the shore. As I reached Wellington Square, a drunk in a Rangers top swayed in front of the car, raised a can of Cally Special towards me in a violent Nazi salute. I watched him for a moment, let the bead of my eye meet his. He stared back. I was close enough to count the lines of the spider's web tattooed on his neck. He took a swig on his tin. I knew what was coming next: a fountain of sticky bear-cum-gob that I'd be scrubbing off my bonnet for days to come.

I killed the engine in an instant, stepped out.

'Do one!'

The yob stalled mid-swig. He dropped his 'brows, looked more Neanderthal than ever.

I let him have a couple of seconds to register his options, took a step closer. 'You testing me, lad?'

The mouthful of beer made his cheeks bulge. Another half-gone hoodie to his left called out, 'Leave it, Davie.'

I dipped a nod in the direction of the second yob; Davie saw sense, spat the mouthful of Special Brew in the gutter and made his way to the side of the road. I kept my eye on them as I returned to the car. There was a time when this kind of encounter would have had my pulse racing. Not now. The force had taught me to face down conflict. These morons needed boundaries or they ran amok. When I was in uniform, an old desk sergeant had told me the trick to dealing with them was sending in the WPCs.

'You ever seen dogs fighting in the street, Doug?' he'd said.

'Aye, of course.'

'Well, you'll know then, the one thing that separates the rowdy males is … a female.'

I laughed. 'I get you.'

He'd winked, tapped the tip of his nose conspiratorially.

'These rough lads are no wiser than dogs, the sight of a woman in uniform has smoke coming out their ears!'

I got back in the car. Fired the ignition and pulled out. After all the years I'd been away, I could still spot the West Coast genes a mile off. The tin-pot hard men, the coat-hanger shoulders poking beneath the Old Firm tops, the ever-handy bottle of ginger or compensatory chib. It was pathetic; made me ashamed to be Scottish. I couldn't believe we were perpetrating the lineage at this point in human development.

I wondered if it would ever change around here.

There'd be more conflict coming my way if I dug into Lyn's troubles. I could count on it. It didn't faze me. But would I be better opting for the quiet life? Something told me that, were I pushed, this town wouldn't know what had hit it. If another ersatz hard man got in my way, I'd burst him like a balloon. It's what I'd become.

The road towards the front was pot-holed, heavily scarred and ramped to death. Did those things make any difference? I doubted it. The boy-racers were still out in force, lined up all the way along the shore; a procession of pimped-up Astras and go-faster Golfs with spotty yoofs at the wheel. I allowed myself a snigger and pulled a left for the breakwater.

The wind was biting, a tang of sea-spray adding to the heady mix as I stepped out. I raised my collar and traced the well-worn steps through the sand hill that had formed on the tarmac surface. Some dog walkers and fishermen were up ahead, but sufficiently far off not to bother me. I didn't feel in the mood for contact.

I remembered coming down this end of town when I was a boy; it held a fascination for youngsters of my generation, but there were none here today. They'd be inside, attached to games consoles no doubt. As I turned towards the sea I took in the filth-strewn beach, blackened logs, ripped nets and sun-worn plastics the mainstay of the assorted flotsam and jetsam. It must have looked like this when I last visited, I just didn't remember it this way. I looked towards the sky; the sun was hiding too.

I let the wind whistle round my ears for a few minutes, then turned back towards the car. I don't know what I'd hoped to find down here; inspiration? Reason, maybe? Whatever, I hadn't found it. As I walked towards the four towers of the Pavilion I let my mind trip back to darker, drunken days when the Piv was a dancehall. It seemed like a million years ago now; Lyn had been there though.

I saw her in a biker's jacket, ripped 501s, and mad spiky hair that came straight from a L'Oreal ad of the time. She was dancing to The Waterboys. At least, that's how I remember her. Were the memories real? At this stage, was anything? Did it matter?

I had to help her. There was no talking myself out of it. There was no talking sense to myself. There was no reason. Someone said once, 'The heart has its reason that reason knows not of.'

I removed my mobile from my inside pocket, scrolled through my contacts as I got into the car.

The number I selected was ringing before I closed the door.

'Hello.'

'Mason ... it's Doug Michie.'

A stall on the line. 'Why in the world are you calling me?'

'Because it's serious.'

Mason took a breath, spoke calmly. 'Well, it would certainly have to be that.'

Chapter 5

I sat at the South Harbour Street lights, waiting on the filter. Two slightly-built youths battled the elements to scrape flaking paint from a manky shop front. It was an old shop, one of the weather-scarred ones that sat at the foot of the Sandgate feeling sorry for themselves. I wanted to get out and help, scrub the place down; the street had become an eyesore. Fine, if I was just another rep or white-van man passing through, but this was my old home town. The heart of Burns Country. I still had some respect for the place, if nobody else did. I trembled at the thought of tourists driving up from the yuppie-developed Shore to be greeted with this. It was an embarrassment to rank alongside finding your grandmother had wandered into town in her nightie.

As the lights changed, and I pulled out, I remembered a pizzeria that used to be down this way when there was still paint on the buildings. Stefano's did a mean thin-crust. I smiled to myself. It didn't last; that was the trouble with coming home, very little was like I remembered it. It used to be easy getting around the Auld Toun. I was old enough to recall the days before the powers-that-be pedestrianised, or should that be paralysed, the High Street. Before a parking voucher scheme no-one could find tickets for. Before Woolies went, and one whole end of the town went with it. I wondered what was next. The new Ayr seemed to be leaving the old Ayr to hang.

I eased past the Carnegie Library, got a break at the second set of lights and swung round past King Street Police Station. The traffic thickened before the roundabout and I found myself applying the brakes. I was staring across at the station when I suddenly felt the blood in my veins shriek. My heart ramped, as I saw a face I recognised exit the front door and walk towards a silver Lexus.

'Gilmour.' The word fell flatly from my lips.

I watched him yank the door of the car open and slam it behind him as he got in, planted the foot. A wail of car horns followed him as he sped onto the roundabout.

Someone was in a hurry.

I waited for the traffic to clear and made a mental note of the scene I'd just observed. Jonny Gilmour hadn't changed much in the last few years; he'd grown thicker round the middle, and his hair was shorter than the old mullet he once wore, but he still had the look of a man you didn't want to get in the way of. He seemed to be doing okay for himself, though, driving a Lexus; I remembered when he had holes in his gutties. He was in and out of the station back then as well.

I let the revs out on John Street, took the roundabout at Dampark onto Station Road and followed the clogged arteries of Auld Ayr all the way to Morrisons. I didn't want anything from there; nothing depressed me more than bumping elbows and knees in overly lit supermarkets, but the Market Bar was located in the top end of the store's car park. I pulled up and made for the door.

The bar had changed little in the years since I'd last got tanked up on Tennent's lager on the way to a night on the town. They kept the place warm, homely. Just how I liked it. I spied Mason straight away, even with his back to me. He was a bear of a man, as broad as he was; the burden of the job looked no more than a chip on his shoulders. I walked over and nodded to the barman to refill his pint, bring me the same.

'Hello, Mason.'

A slow creak emitted from his chair as he turned. 'Doug.'

I moved myself to the other side of the table, sat facing him. There was a gap of a few seconds before I spoke again. 'You look well, haven't changed.'

'Spare me the small chat, eh?'

I looked up as our pints arrived. 'Okay.'

Mason nodded to the barman, almost smiled. 'So, to what do I owe the pleasure?'

There didn't seem any point dressing it up. Mason knew me, had done for years. We'd been in uniform together. Seen things. Shared experience, they called it. Some of those experiences we'd sooner forget; most, to be honest, but they counted for something. They brought weight to the table and Mason knew that as well as I did.

'I'm back in town.'

'I see that.'

'Aye, well, I'm not here for old time's sake … you needn't worry about that.'

He raised a hand and planted it on the table. The pints trembled; some golden liquid escaped over the brim of my glass. 'What do you want, Doug?'

I wiped the table with a beer mat, took a sip of my pint. 'A friend of mine, her son's in trouble.'

'A friend?'

'That's right.'

'What kind of trouble?'

I lowered my glass, peered over the brim. 'The worst kind.'

'And you're telling me this, why?'

I pressed my back firmly into the chair, exhaled. 'Come on, Mason, don't make me go over old ground.'

A laugh, his face reddened. 'God Almighty, Doug, are you still playing that tune?'

I knew what he meant, but acted dumb. 'What?'

'The old pal's act ... it doesn't wash these days.' Mason shook his head, sucked in his mouth. Two yellowed teeth dug into the fleshy part of his lower lip. 'You know that, Doug ... not now, it's all changed, the world we live in.'

My jaw tightened. 'We haven't.'

He looked away. Shook his head again.

I spoke louder. 'I said, we haven't changed, Mason.'

'Speak for yourself.' He looked edgy, started to claw at a packet of Embassy Regal that sat on the table in front of him.

'We still know right from wrong, don't we?' I didn't give him time to answer, leaned forward and let the tone of my voice be his guide. 'My friend's name is Lyn McPherson. Her son is called Glenn and he's been charged with murder. Now I don't know the ins and outs of it, but I've been around long enough to know when something's not right.'

Mason pocketed the cigarettes, rose. 'I'm promising nothing. Do you hear me, Doug?'

I nodded.

Mason started to fasten his jacket. 'I'll take a look. But we don't meet like this again, do you hear me?'

I nodded. Got up to face him. 'One more thing ...'

He rolled his eyes. 'What now?'

I lowered my voice, spoke to his lapels. 'I saw an old face today. Jonny Gilmour.'

Mason put his hands in his pockets, shrugged. I let the name float in the air for a few moments, then tried to discern what I could from his expression. Nothing came.

I spoke again. 'He was at the station. Looked riled.'

Mason's head shifted, left to right. He took a deep breath. 'Don't be picking at old wounds, Doug ... that wouldn't be very wise where Gilmour's concerned.'

Chapter 6

The room was familiar, but then, why wouldn't it be? I'd spent the first twenty-or-so years of my life here. New wallpaper came and went, at least a couple of times, but the florid seventies swirl-print that had been up when I was a lad stayed with me. It was likely still there, under a layer of woodchip or two. Some memories of screaming matches with my parents trapped with it, maybe the theme tune to Kojak or On the Buses playing in the background. Days long gone. I raised myself on the edge of the bed; the ageing springs creaked beneath me, made me wonder about my own mortality. My second night in my mother's home felt like a siren's wail to throw myself at the all-too-recognisable wall. I resisted, for now.

I stood staring at the single bed I'd slept in; it was crammed against the wall. A functional cabinet, lamp atop, sat beside it. I remembered sick days from school I'd spent sitting up in this bed, reading the Beano and the Dandy, maybe a new copy of Shoot if I'd been running a temperature. It seemed so long ago, like looking back on a world that only existed in black and white pictures now. I knew that coming home to Ayr would stir up some memories, but I wasn't prepared for the concomitant emotional response. I felt like I was revising for an exam on a part of my life that

I'd previously forgotten about. It seemed so alien to me now, after the force, after Ulster.

I removed my Levi's from the old Corby trouser press that belonged to my late father; a lot of his possessions seemed to be migrating to parts of the house he never inhabited. It was like he was being pushed out, at least, it seemed that way to me. I wondered why my mother still stayed here; she inhabited the place like a ghost. It was too big for her; a family home needed a family. She knew that too, but she was living in the past. Could I fault her for that? Didn't we all?

I flung on a crisp white T-shirt, black V-neck. Laced my boots and made for the kitchen. On the stairs I smelt the Berkeley menthols my mother smoked; she was up and about, clinking glasses in the sink. As I walked in she pinched her lips tightly around the cigarette's filter tip, the long ash threatening to fall on the floor as she spoke. 'You're up early.'

I nodded. There was a glass of port sitting behind her. 'Not starting as early as some.'

She turned away from me, walked towards the glass. Her cigarette ash fell as she placed the Berkeley in the ashtray. The small port went with her as she left the kitchen, mumbling something I never cared to discern.

I shook my head as the door closed.

Shaking my head at my mother wasn't an altogether new response. I put on my jacket and picked up the dog's lead, called, 'Ben ... Ben ...'

The dog meandered his way from the dining room into the kitchen. The clack of his long claws on the floor tiles told me he wasn't getting walked as much as he should. He stumbled, caught the corner of the fridge with his head; he was aging too, losing his sight.

'Come on boy, let's get you some air, eh?'

I took down my jacket, checked my mobile phone was in the pocket. There was a missed call; I didn't recognise the number. It struck me that it might be Lyn, or maybe Mason. I doubted the latter; he would make me wait. Mason didn't want me on his patch; he didn't want the grief. He was counting his days till retirement, and counting on them all being easy. I couldn't blame him; we'd both had our fair share of hard days for sure.

The lab's coat was illuminated in the brightness of the morning sun: grey and white flecks showing down his spine and around his ears. I still remembered him as a pup, a small black bundle – a surrogate child that never fully met the need. He'd let my mother down because he'd failed to live up to her expectations, but hadn't we all? She had never worked, had a career, she was a mother and when we grew up, left her, that was it. Life stopped. I don't think I had fully understood this until recently; leaving the force had left me empty too. All those years, all that commitment, it defined me. But now it was gone. Over.

The dog was bumping into walls, left and right. I tightened the lead. In the daylight, his milky-blue cataracts were more visible. The sight of him wounded me, made me want to hit out at the injustice. But it was only nature. I knew you couldn't fight it.

'Come on, Ben ...'

He wagged his old tail.

'Good lad.'

The neighbourhood was quiet; this part of town – the edge of Alloway – always was now. It hadn't always been that way. I knew it when there were families, young children in the neatly appointed homes. Not even two salaries could afford them now; not even the economic crash helped. The place was becoming an extension of God's waiting room, old widows and widowers pottering about and eyeing the street through twitching curtains. Few ventured outside; they no longer had the energy to maintain gardens. The council seemed to have abandoned the roads; grassy areas were left unattended. All life seemed to have been sucked out of the place.

I came off the Maybole Road and down Lauchlanglen, crossed into Rozelle. Ben was struggling now, his arthritic hips dragging behind him. I slowed the pace as we left the pavement and took the wooded path. I had a circuit route in mind that would get us back to my mother's house; I just hoped I wasn't going to have to carry the dog the last part of the way. Neither of us would like that.

I felt the phone in my pocket and knew I needed to return the call.

Dialled.

Ringing.

'Hello ...' It was Lyn.

'I got your call.'

A pause; she seemed to be processing my response. 'Oh yeah, I just wanted to ask if you had, y'know ...'

She was reaching. Desperate for any news. 'Lyn, it's too soon.'

Her tone softened, lowered. 'I thought so.'

'Look, I've made some ... enquiries.'

'I see.' I could sense the disappointment in her tone.

I tried to enliven my own voice. 'But, there's still plenty we can be getting on with.'

I waited for a reply. None came.

I said, 'I need you to make a list of Glenn's friends for me, people he knew, worked with and so on ...'

'Why?'

That was the question. 'So I can speak to them.' I needed to get a picture of who her son was, what kind of person he was. But there was more besides. 'And Kirsty ... can you put me in touch with her people?'

Lyn stalled, 'I–I don't know.'

I was a cop, once. I knew most murder victims knew their killer. 'It's important.'

'Do you mean her parents?' said Lyn.

'Yes ... among others.'

'Well, it's just that ...' the line fizzed, then stilled to silence.

'Lyn ... is there something you have to tell me?'

The line crackled some more, then: 'Before you go speaking to Kirsty's parents, Doug.' A sigh; her voice quivered. 'I think there's something I should tell you.'

Chapter 7

I returned home to find my mother asleep on the couch. Near comatose would be a more accurate description. The television blared in the background – Jeremy Kyle lording it over his latter-day bear-pit. I picked up the doofer, flicked it to off. My mother barely stirred, her mouth agape as her head rested on the arm of the couch. I leant over to straighten the upturned bottle of port that lay on the floor. It was empty. Not a drop had escaped her lips.

I shook my head.

This was my mother, and she was out of it.

I could hardly judge; I'd had my fair share of days on the sauce. But they were behind me. I realised long ago that the road of excess never led to the palace of wisdom. The road of excess led to the road of excess.

I heard the dog clatter into the door behind me, moved to lay a hand on his ear, reassure him.

'There, boy …' I turned him around, led him from the sitting room towards the kitchen and closed the door behind us.

I knew I wasn't going to be able to stay with my mother. I had known that before I left Ulster, but somehow thought I might manage a few days whilst I got myself set up in Ayr. She had always liked a drink, my mam. Had always liked a rant, getting it all off her chest. They were the worst kind of drinkers, the morose. They used inebriation as an excuse to vent their anger at life's misfortunes. My mother seemed to have gone passed that stage now; reached the point where burning energy on anger wasn't an option when her reserves were so low. She drank for the release of oblivion.

I took the phone from the kitchen wall, dialled my sister's number. Claire had left the Auld Toun too, was holed up in the wilds in Inverness with a husband and a clutch of kids. I never envied her, perhaps because she never seemed in the remotest neighbourhood of happy.

I dialled.

Ringing.

An answer phone. The classic, 'Please leave a message after the tone.'

I took a shallow breath. 'Claire, it's Doug ... I just got back home, to Ayr. I think we need to talk about Mam ...'

I left my mobile number and hung up.

I watched Ben lap at his bowl of water. He was tired, nosing the edge of the bowl with his drooping face. When he was sated, the old dog staggered towards his basket in the corner of the room and threw himself down. I decided he needed rest, or perhaps knew the routine now. Either way, I let them sleep it off, headed back for the front door.

On the Maybole Road I walked with a vague intention of paying a visit to an old contact from my days in uniform. I didn't know if Veitch would be at home, or even in the same house. It didn't matter. I felt like walking; it let me think. What I'd mostly been thinking of lately was Mason's reaction to my mention of Jonny Gilmour. Something unsettled me about my sighting of Gilmour at the police station and Mason's warning to steer clear only confirmed my suspicions. It might have nothing to do with the case but instinct told me Gilmour was up to no good, and that I was onto something.

There were leaves blowing on the road, filling up gardens and clogging gutters. This time of year always felt like a point of stasis to me: like something was waiting to happen. I hadn't come home to Ayr hoping to fill my days with the same kind of duty I had left in the north of Ireland, but it had found me. I steeled myself for what was ahead; I knew Lyn needed me, needed my help, though something told me she wasn't about to reveal the full picture just yet. I knew it would be up to me to pull it into focus.

I passed what had once been a nursing home; it had been replaced with a block of flats. In front of the flats sat a Tesco Express where the old Anfield Hotel once stood. I don't know if the Anfield ever took paying guests. I only knew the lounge bar. The country and western singer Sidney Divine had once owned it, put pictures of himself on the walls. I smiled to myself remembering the pints he poured me, and how I'd laughed at his appearances on Scotch & Wry alongside Rikki Fulton. The Tesco Express couldn't obliterate those memories.

The rain started as I rounded the corner, passed under the railway arch and made my way across the playing fields to Kincaidston. When I was in uniform, they called the place Zulu. I never thought it deserved the reputation. There were good people living there alongside the scrotes. Veitch, when I knew him, fell into the latter category. Mason and myself had pulled him for a badger baiting escapade up the Carrick Hills. We were both wild in those days, knew a prosecution was a long-shot, so we gave him a hiding he would never forget. As I stood outside his front door, I hoped his memory was intact.

'Hello, Veitchy.'

'What the …' He eyed me up and down, seemed to be coming out of a stoner's stupor.

I pushed passed him into the hallway.

'Hey, hey … what's this all about?'

I surveyed the premises, found the place empty. In the living room an ashtray overflowed with cigarette dowps, and Rizzla papers. A fat block of Moroccan sat by a packet of Regal Kingsize. I picked it up.

'What's this?'

He girned, 'A wee bit of puff … you still polis, eh?'

'I'll ask the questions, Veitchy.'

He shook his head; his craggy jaw turned a chin of white bristles towards me. He had aged since we'd last met. I couldn't believe how he'd aged. 'Well this isnae a social call,' he bleated.

'Got that right.'

His eyes followed the block of cannabis resin in my hand. I played with it, toss and catch. 'Although … I did see a glimpse of a friend of yours the other day, got me thinking.'

'A friend ay mine? Who?'

I pocketed the resin. 'Jonny Gilmour.'

Veitch's face creased; deep furrowed lines appeared round the corners of his mouth. His cheeks looked more hollowed now, his brow more furrowed. It was a look of stupefaction, at least that's what he wanted me to believe; I went with a wiser assessment of Rabbie's: *suspicion is a heavy armour and with its weight it impedes more than it protects.*

'Haven't seen him in a month ay Sundays,' Veitch protested.

I smiled, 'That right?'

'Sure ay it. Couldn't tell you the last time I saw him, must have been when Adam was a boy …'

I didn't rate his reaction, didn't seem genuine to me. I said, 'You haven't changed house in twenty years, Veitchy. Am I supposed to believe you've changed your muckers?'

'Look, I don't hang about with Jonny Gilmour. I'm

telling you that straight.' His tone was hard, certain. I didn't believe a word of it.

'I think you protest too much, Veitchy.'

'Eh? What's that supposed to mean? Some kind ay riddle or that?'

I turned towards him, closed down the two paces between us and planted a firm index finger in his bony chest. 'There must be something up with your memory, son ... Don't you remember my aversion to lying scrotes?'

He withdrew his head. 'Well, I might have seen him in the passing, now and again like, at the snooker and that.'

'That's better. Carry on.'

Veitch rubbed at the stubble on his chin. 'But he's not exactly what you'd call a mate these days ...'

I dipped my head, towards his face. It was enough.

'Well, look what do you want to know?'

'Everything, Veitchy. Everything ...'

Chapter 8

My mother was just coming round as I dropped the holdall on the living room floor. The noise the bag made was louder than I had intended; the normal reaction for someone waking from sleep would have been a flinch but she didn't stir. A moment or two passed and then suddenly a dim flicker of recognition entered her eyes.

'You're back,' she said.

I didn't know what she meant: back from my walk? Back from Ulster? There was no way of telling what stage of addled she was in. I made a long stare towards the bottle of port, registered grim disapproval on my face, said, 'So, how long have you been hitting the bottle like this?'

Headshakes. 'Oh, spare me …' She sat upright, leaned forward balancing her elbows on her knees. My mother started to gouge at her eyeballs with her knuckles.

'Well?' I dropped in enough intonation to let my feelings sing.

'Don't start on me, son.' The word son was a starter for ten, designed to put me in my place, designed to let me know she had some rank on me. I knew all about rank and it didn't faze me now.

I pointed a finger. 'Look, Mam, I've dived to the bottom of many a bottle myself and I know there's no answers there.'

She let out a laugh. 'Answers … what makes you think I'm looking for them.'

I felt my pulse quicken for an instant, then as quickly as it had risen, it subsided. An immense calm settled over me. It was one of those moments, not quite déjà vu, but in the ballpark, as the Americans say. It takes a drinker to fully comprehend the kind of wisdom she was imparting and it struck me like a hammer blow: my mother's problems were worse than I thought. She wasn't drinking to forget, or to find something; she was drinking for the release of oblivion, an escape from life. I knew this because I had been there; I also knew there was only one escape from this life and alcohol was a poor substitute for it.

I picked up my bag. 'I'll be in touch.'

My mother waved a hand over her head. It was a desultory gesture. I stood staring at her for a moment longer, hunched and broken before me, but it scalded my heart too much. I raised the holdall on my shoulder and headed for the car.

The air outside was crisp and fresh, a low winter sun sitting in the pale-blue sky. The leaves clogging the streets were coated in a grey dusting of frost; they huddled against the house fronts and garden walls like jagged buttresses. When I was a boy, I liked this time of year; it signalled the run-up to Christmas, to presents and parties. It had been a long time since I had remembered those feelings of untrammelled joy; I knew they were still in me, but today they seemed buried beyond any evisceration I could imagine.

I unlocked the Audi, got in and started the engine. The TT purred as I pumped the pedal and pulled out onto the road. I drove towards the A77; the car needed a short burn to let out some grunt. The road was busy, lots of 4x4 Doonfoot tractors on the school run. I spotted one with an Ayr number plate, had a little smile to myself: it was heading back towards Alloway – but weren't they all?

At the Whittlets Roundabout I exited at the gym and followed the road back into town on auto-pilot. I knew where I was headed, knew what I had to do. I had driven past the guest houses on Queens Terrace a couple of times on this visit already; was I subconsciously planning to hole up there at the time? I didn't doubt it – so many of my choices seemed to be pre-programmed these days that I felt like an actor in my own life.

I had picked out the place I wanted to stay; it was at the far end, next to the court. As I pulled up I noticed a sign on the outside wall which read: licensed to residents. I didn't think I had seen this before; at least, I hadn't registered it. Still, it dug at my conscience after the lecture I'd given my mother.

I made my way inside, lowered my bag at the front desk and looked about. A woman in her bad fifties wearing a tabard was at work with a Henry hoover. She spotted me and made her way over to the front desk with a slow gait.

'Yes?' she said.

'I'd like a room.'

'Long or short stay?'

I didn't know the answer to that, shrugged.

She put on a pair of glasses that sat round her neck on a chain, looked me up and down. 'We don't take people on benefits …'

'I'll pay cash.'

She twisted her mouth, seemed to doubt me. 'Name?'

'Doug Michie.'

As she scratched my details in a big brown ledger I watched the Biro's nib execute her intricate copper-plate.

'You have beautiful handwriting.'

She never turned a hair; handed me a key attached to a long plastic slab that could have doubled as a doorstop. 'Room 7 … upstairs on the left.'

'Is there a view?'

She sneered. I went for broke. 'There wouldn't be a Jacuzzi on the premises?'

The glasses came off, the hoover went on. I didn't get an answer.

I carried my bag up to my room by myself. The view was of the back close; if I raised myself on tiptoes I could see the sometime crazy golf course. I opened the window, let out the musty air. My test of the bedsprings was answered with a rusty squeak. I patted the back of the room's one chair and evacuated a cloud of dusty effluvia that started me coughing. I grabbed a glass from the side of the sink; it was wrapped in hard white tissue paper, the kind we used to trace with at school. The glass inside – after a million washes – was almost opaque with scratches. I filled it with water and took a slow draft. My throat soothed instantly and I felt my mind still.

I looked around the grim room. Registered the Nylon bedspread. The Gideon's Bible. The patched carpet. The faded print of a crying girl being comforted by a Lassie dog. So, this was home for the short term. I shook my head and lowered myself slowly onto the bed.

If this was home, then I was here for a reason and I knew what that was. I removed my mobile phone from my pocket and opened my email. A list of names I'd requested had come in. I scanned them; none meant anything to me, but they might soon. Glaring by their absence, however, were some names that I definitely had to query.

I closed down the email. Dialled a number.

Ringing.

'Hello …'

'Hello, Lyn …'

'Doug.' Her voice was high, hopeful. 'Have you heard anything?'

I felt the edges of my mouth tighten into a grimace.

'You'd be the first to know.'

A pause, reality flooding back in. Then, 'I take it you got the list I sent.'

'I did, yeah ... but why aren't Kirsty's parents on there?'

Her voice trembled, 'I want to let sleeping dog's lie.'

I didn't buy it, not for a second. 'Lyn, their daughter has been killed. There's no way I can conduct an investigation into Kirsty's death without talking to her parents.'

'I just want to leave them be ...'

I registered the emotion behind her chant. 'Lyn, it's in their benefit to speak to me too, you know that.'

'I know! But, I just want them left alone. Please, Doug, you have to understand ...'

I understood.

'When we last spoke about Kirsty's people you said you had something to tell me ...'

She cleared her throat. 'I know ...'

'And?'

Her tone changed, became lighter. It was as if she had practiced a response. 'Where are you?'

I straightened my back. 'I'm in Ayr ... in a guest house.'

'Where?'

'Down the front ... Queens Terrace.'

'I know it. I'll meet you at the Horizon Hotel in an hour. Can you make that?'

I stood up, walked towards the window. It was raining again.

'One hour ... with answers, Lyn.'

Chapter 9

The rain was back. That familiar, insidious drizzle that felt light enough to sit on the air. I walked a few steps down Queens Terrace towards the port with my head dipped to the pavement. By the end of the street I was brushing a heavy layer of moisture from my shoulders. The wind seemed to be soughing out at sea, whispering across the sand. I turned my ear to catch the ghost of a voice drifting up from the beach – it was a haunting roar – but as I stalled I caught sight of a walker. She was roaring after a runaway dog.

I felt on edge, and I knew why.

I'd taken on a case, my first since leaving the force. But it wasn't any case; it wasn't a missing persons or an errant husband playing away from home. I'd agreed to look into a murder. As the days stretched out, however, I had started to wonder what I was really doing.

It wasn't the simple fact that I was back in Ayr, my old home town, where there were ghosts everywhere, it was the unshakeable fear that all was not as it seemed. I'd learned to trust the nagging, gnawing voices that accompanied an investigation: they were there for a reason, but right now they were being bawled out by an opposing set of voices. Auld Ayr meant more to me than I had assumed. It was more than the town of my childhood, my youth. I had grown up here, there was a part of the place that I carried with me wherever I went: the town, its people – they had formed me. I couldn't escape that. It was a visceral identification and it stirred deep inside me. I wondered if Lyn saw this.

I reached the end of the terrace, turned the corner, bracing myself against a blast of sand-filled wind. I stepped on some blue mussel shells dropped by the circling gulls. They cracked like gunshots underfoot.

The Horizon Hotel had changed since I last saw it, but so had a lot of the town. I stepped inside. Soft furnishings and mood lighting greeted me. The smooth-lined fixtures and fittings looked neat and clean, too clinical for the purpose of my visit. I spotted Lyn seated on a leather sofa by the wall; she seemed distant. I nodded to the barman and made my way towards the other side of the friendly room.

'Hello, Lyn.'

She started. 'Oh, hi.'

The barman came. I ordered a coffee. 'Are you okay, Lyn?'

She smiled. 'Yes, fine.' She was lying. In my racket, you learn the cues early.

Lyn reached into her bag, removed a few sheaves of paper. 'I thought I'd print out the list you wanted.'

I took the contacts of Glenn's known associates, turned it over. It felt too soon to bring up what I had on my mind, but I'd never been very good at keeping a lid on things. 'And, Kirsty's parents: are they on there now?'

Lyn bit her lip, jerked her head towards the window. The sea beyond had started to turn nasty. White rollers frothed, battered at the beach. 'I–I … look, the thing is …'

I decided to make it simple for her. 'Without the parents the investigation is dead in the water.'

She jerked back from the window, her eyes widening. 'What?'

I had attracted her attention, got her focus. It was where I wanted her. 'It's like this, Lyn: their daughter was murdered, and they knew things about Kirsty that no-one else did. They're holding important information and I need to access it.'

'But …'

'Lyn, it would be easy for me to find them, pay them a visit. Only, I'm not doing this for me, I'm doing it for you, and for Glenn. If you don't want me to, then we go no further.'

'What are you saying, Doug?' Her stare intensified. She seemed to lock into my thoughts.

'I'm saying, we have to do this my way. I'm saying, you have to trust me.'

Lyn touched the edge of her mouth. I noticed the cherry-coloured polish on her nails had chipped. For a moment she was still, then she dipped her hand into her bag and removed a pen, took up the paper once more.

'This is Frank and Sheila's address … they stay out on the Dunure Road. They're good people, nice people …'

I knew she was stalling, holding back. '*But?*'

Her lips pursed. 'They never liked Glenn.'

I lowered my voice. 'Why?'

'There was one or two … incidents.'

'Go on …'

Lyn turned back to face the window. 'Glenn had a hot head,' she sighed, 'took that from his father, but he was a good boy. He would never harm anyone and he loved Kirsty.' She turned to face me. 'I know that.'

'Okay.' I watched Lyn's eyes moisten; her complexion lost some of its colour. 'So why the animosity from her parents towards Glenn?'

She shook her head. Her shoulders drooped. 'I don't know, I really don't. I think it was as simple as they never thought he was good enough for their daughter ... he was from a broken home. He didn't work and Kirsty did ... she was their little princess.'

I knew I wasn't getting the full story. 'And this hot head of Glenn's wouldn't help.'

She bit. 'He never harmed her. Never harmed a hair on her head ... you have to believe that!'

I saw the ice in her glare. 'Okay. But you said yourself that they rowed.'

'They were kids. Come on, Doug, remember what we were like at that age? Fought like cat and dog because we didn't know any better.' She leaned forward, stretched her hand out and took mine. 'You know I'm right. We needed time to learn how to get along with each other but we never gave ourselves the chance. Doug, we were too young to know any better.'

I looked down at our hands, entwined. Every instinct I had wailed at me to get up and walk. Back through the door. Back to the guest house. Back to my life. *My* life, not the one I thought I was living.

'Lyn, this isn't about us,' I said.

She firmed her grip. I was close enough to see the flecks of grey in her dark brown eyes. 'We never gave *us* a chance, Doug. Not a chance.'

Chapter 10

What Veitchy had told me about Jonny Gilmour could have filled the back of a postage stamp. A particularly small postage stamp. By contrast he'd been voluminous in his praise of him, and that, coupled with my sighting of Gilmour at the King Street police station was enough to set my antennae twitching. Once he was warmed up, Veitchy had played to type – his type being the tin-pot hard man that the west of Scotland pushed out like paving weeds. He liked to be known as a player in the Auld Toun but he was just another bottom feeder. A scrote. His status was garnered from close alignment to bigger fish: those like Gilmour.

The pair had started out as football casuals but that was just a front, a vent for Gilmour's psychopathic tendencies; Veitchy went along to soak in the testosterone-filled air and hope some kind of rep' brushed off on him. In a way it did: Mason and myself certainly got to know him. He was what we called a ferret back then, the type of contact that was so easy to lean on, to manipulate, that you could flush names out of him. A ferret like that has a short shelf-life though; scrotes soon know to keep their traps shut around them.

Veitchy had been of some use to me though. He'd let slip that Gilmour liked to hold court at the Davis Snooker Club over at Tam's Brig. I knew the place; in my day it had been the antidote to The Bobby's snooker hall. I remembered The Bobby's fondly; the broad, dark hall had something that seemed in the process of being scrubbed from the new Ayr: atmosphere. It was a place for patter, for passing the night somewhere other than the pub. It was a bloke-ish domain. A million miles from the trendy coffee houses and super pubs that filled the place now. As I fell into reverie, I saw how far the town had come, but wondered about the direction.

I checked my watch; I'd been in place for the best part of an hour. This was the low-glamour end of detective work. The American TV cops called it stakeout – a surprisingly sprightly name for freezing your backside off in a car park at night. Jonny Gilmour's silver Lexus sat to the far left of the car park. I had the private reg' – surprisingly not one containing Ayr – in sight. On the driver's seat I had a camera with a telephoto lens; I doubted there was enough light to take decent shots, but I'd get a good view of Gilmour when he showed and that might tell me something. I knew if I had to rely on Veitchy, or Mason for that matter, that I'd be waiting a long time.

I lit a Regal, rolled down the window. It was the first of a new pack that I'd bought from a shop down the shore and it tasted a little funny.

'What the?' I looked at the tip of the cigarette; it was burning quickly, the paper turning brown half-way up the underside of the cig. I took another quick drag. If this was a Regal, I was Ruud Gullit. I flicked the filter tip into the night. A hail of amber sparks showered the tarmac.

I removed the pack from my pocket, checked the side. The Government health warning was there, but it looked smaller than I remembered. 'Out of date?' I was murmuring to myself, going stir crazy in the cold of the car, when suddenly the sound of footfalls alerted me to raise the camera.

It was Gilmour. There was a smaller man with him, grey suit and a navy-blue tie that was loosened round his neck. He looked corporate and quite well-to-do. He wasn't on the lower rungs of the ladder that was for sure. The pair seemed to be relaxed in each others company, though, starting off a mock light-sabre fight with their cue cases.

'Very friendly boys,' I muttered, before firing a comment of Rabbie's at Gilmour: *'wretched is the person who hangs on by the favours of the powerful.'*

I battered off a few pictures. The more I focussed the lens on the suit, the more he seemed familiar to me. He wasn't police. At least, he wasn't any kind of police I recognised. He might have been a desk jockey or a bean counter. But I steered clear of that lot. The thought struck me: maybe I wouldn't be sitting in a grimy Ayr car park scoping scrotes if I'd paid more attention to the suits who ran the RUC. I pushed Ulster from my mind; I needed to keep my thoughts clear, my mind open and alert.

The pair got into the Lexus, drove off. I turned the ignition on the TT, pulled out. I let them get past the roundabout, watched them head for Prestwick and then let out the clutch and followed at a proper distance.

'Okay, Gilmour … lead the way.'

A thought jumped at me: you might be wasting your time, Doug. I nodded it down. Sure, I could be. But something told me I was onto something with Gilmour. Mason's reaction was writ large in my mind. He warned me away. He was never a man for subtleties, our Mason, but he knew how the job got done.

'What were you hinting at, Mason?' I was still mumbling to myself, still airing my thoughts when the Lexus pulled over and stopped outside a villa on the Prestwick Road. It was one of the old red sandstone jobs, I'd be guessing four bedrooms at least, kind that attracted a tidy price tag.

The suit got out the car, raised his cue case and put up his collar as he jogged up the drive.

Gilmour tapped the horn twice and pulled out.

I followed on.

Prestwick town had changed, seemed busier. Seemed even further down the path to yuppie-dom than Ayr. The pubs looked to be doing good trade, plenty of teenage girls teetering on vertiginous heels. The sight of them put a knot in my stomach. Kirsty wasn't much older than them. She was too young. The loss of such a young life was a wrong that enraged me, but the way she had gone made my fists grip the wheel tighter.

At The Dome I looked in the big windows, thought of the roaring fire they lit during the winter months. Gilmour had beat the lights, headed for the Cross. I followed on, past The Red Lion on my left and made for the Monkton Roundabout. The Lexus driver had other plans though, veered to the slip road on the left, headed for Troon. I dropped the gears, snuck in behind a Micra and watched the car in front.

We hadn't gone far when the blinkers started and Gilmour pulled in to a gated driveway. I clocked the number on the white stanchion out front, then drove past, slowed my speed and stopped. As I turned in my seat I had just enough time to catch Gilmour pulling up outside a dreary looking, overly lit mansion.

Jesus, Jonny Boy, you've come a long way in a short time ... From council curtains to Southwoods.

Chapter 11

I dropped the revs on the TT, slipped down the gears and flicked the blinkers on. It seemed an overly cautious trip to be taking, but Mason insisted. I hadn't been out this way, save passing through, for some time. A host of McMansions had sprouted up on the other side of the road from the entrance to Belleisle golf club. An overt display of wealth, incongruous with the news full of nations facing bankruptcy. I thinned my eyes, allowed a squint towards the bricks and mortar someone had mortgaged their life to: what was the point? Money, greed, it had taken over. Everywhere. This was Ayrshire. I still remembered the Thatcher years. The pit closures and how the miners fought, in the end, for nothing. They closed the pits anyway. The miners got a few bob, but that was cold comfort for having their way of life taken from them. The money went fast – six-month millionaires they called them; I wondered if they felt right having it. Some of us still held onto values you couldn't measure in pound signs.

The car park was half empty; I was sure it wasn't half full. As I pulled up outside what had once been a popular café and 19th hole I clocked the decay of years. I had to double take. There didn't seem to have been enough time for this level of ruin to take hold. I looked around.

The place had once been full of people; dog-walkers, children playing. It was surprising how quickly they'd disappeared. Abandoned the place. I wanted to join them.

I spotted Mason's car in the bays at the far end of the enclosure and looked around for him. There was no sign. He'd told me: 'On the dot. By the cages. I won't hang around.'

I knew where he meant. I'd taken my sister's kids to see the animals they kept there: small animals – rabbits and birds. But as I passed the derelict summerhouse with its crumbling structure and dirt-blackened windows, I doubted my chances of seeing anything resembling life that wasn't a weed.

Mason was drawing on a cigarette, his collar raised around his beefy neck. He eyed me momentarily then walked towards the wooded path.

I caught him up. 'I see why you brought me here.'

He turned, bit the tip of his fag. 'Like the grave.'

'You'd see more folk in a graveyard.'

He knitted his brow, brushed some stray cigarette ash from his sleeve and flicked his dowp towards the gutter. 'Let's walk.'

I nodded, opened a palm. 'After you.'

As we went I felt my own cravings ignite, reached into my pocket and removed my Regal Kingsize. It was the same pack I had turned to earlier. The tobacco strayed from the tip of the paper. I shook my head. 'Oh, man …'

Mason tilted his face, raised an eyebrow as he took in the pack. 'Hmnn.'

I lifted the cigarettes. 'They're fakes, you know.'

'Oh, I know. You obviously didn't.' He allowed himself a smile. Two rows of teeth stained with coffee and nicotine on display.

'Local problem is it?' I held up the pack as I spoke. I couldn't believe things had got so bad here that there was a black market in knock-off ciggies. What was next? Razor blades? Pretty Pollys? It was like 1944 all over again. 'Are you not doing anything about it?'

Mason lunged for the pack, scrunched it in his great mitt, said, 'Excise isn't my department, Doug!'

I bit. 'Flogging them in your manor is?'

He shook his head. The extra collars round his neck quivered as he moved. 'I'll give you one of mine … if it'll shut you up.'

I accepted. Lit up. Could see it was time to change subject. 'Okay, so why am I here?'

Mason retrieved the lighter he'd given me, put his hands back in his pockets and turned to face the path. A pile of damp leaves blocked our way as we progressed. He raised himself on his toes, momentarily, then kicked the obstruction away like a rugby ball. His cheeks flushed slightly with the exertion. 'Well, not because you asked me, for sure.'

'Oh, really.'

He turned, his nostrils flared. 'Yes, really, Doug.' He lifted a finger, wagged it at me as he spoke through those stained teeth. He looked fierce. 'I've been doing some digging, on you … mate.'

'Oh yeah, better watch that. I hear it gives you dirty hands.'

Mason recoiled. Forced a laugh. 'From what I hear, you're the one with dirty hands, boy.'

'That right?'

'Yes that's right!' The finger was back, wagging, pointing. 'Not exactly flavour of the month in Ulster are you?'

I felt my chest inflate. He'd done more digging than he had call to. We'd been friends, once. 'You've been busy.'

'Yes, I have … and it's a good job.'

I drew the tip of the cigarette to my lips, inhaled. I held the smoke for a moment, then slowly blew it out, white against the still air. 'You should take all you hear with a pinch of salt, Mason. You know as well as me that you make precious few friends in this racket.'

'By the sounds of things you made quite a round number … zero.' I wondered who he'd been talking to, but found I didn't really care. Ulster and the RUC was behind me. I'd moved on. There was nothing there that could harm me here, unless I let it.

'Okay, Mason, you've made your point. But we're not in Ulster.'

The corners of his eyes creased; his lids slanted as he looked at me through narrow slits. 'No. You've missed the point. I'm warning you, I don't want you repeating your old mistakes on my patch.'

I played it cool, tried to laugh him off. 'And what makes you think I'd do that?'

He grabbed me by the shoulders, pressed me hard into a tree. I wasn't expecting it and as my hands fell, the cigarette floated to the ground. I was pinned there, stuck.

Mason spoke, 'Ulster wasn't the only place I did some digging. I did plenty close to home too.'

'Will you get off me?' I kept my voice low. But my heart was pounding. A rage building in me.

'Kirsty Donald … favour for a friend, an old friend, is it?'

I struggled to free myself, bit the inside of my cheek. I tasted blood in my mouth. 'Get your hands off me Mason, I'm warning you.'

He tightened his grip on me, pressed his chest closer to mine. His full weight held me back. I was close enough to feel the spray of his words on my face. 'That girl's file has alarm bells on it! The type that go off in the station when mugs like me start asking questions … What's going on, Doug? I want to know what's going on with Kirsty Donald's murder because some heavy people are taking an interest. And I don't like that … not one bit.'

Chapter 12

I was rattled. Being roughed up by an old friend will have that affect on you. I didn't know where Mason was coming from but his revelations had put a scare on me. Someone, other than me, was taking an interest in the murder of Kirsty Donald. One thing that my meeting with Mason had yielded in my favour, though, was that I'd succeeded in re-igniting his sense of justice. At least, that's what I told myself. Closer to the truth, I'd merely lit his passion not to be outdone. If someone in the station was stamping on toes, he was going to find out who, and why. I turned down the radio in the car; I needed a clear head to think. This ran deeper than I had imagined.

The road was wet out to the Dunure Road, and the Donalds' family home. I'd done my fair share of death knocks in my time on the force, but there was something about lobbing up at the home of a recently bereaved family that still smacked at me. It was never pleasant, never welcome. I wanted to help Lyn find the truth of her son's involvement in Kirsty's murder, but the further I went with the case, the more doubts I had.

As I pulled into Dunure Road the rain was subsiding. I located the house number quickly, parked up and got out the TT. There was a light spray on the breeze – a susurration from the sea. Compared to the battering of rain and gales of late it felt almost a comfort. I flicked the central-locking and turned away from the vehicle towards the house. The garden was strewn with leaves, a bird-table had been upended. Some more leaves had accumulated under the fallen eaves of the bird-table's roof. They'd been there for some time.

I shunned the doorbell and knocked, gently.

A dark figure appeared beyond the frosted glass, seemed to stall for a moment or two, then proceeded towards the door. I heard a key turning in a Yale lock, a slim chain removed. As the door edged open a few inches a whey-faced man in his fifties thinned eyes at me.

'Yes …'

'Mr Donald?'

The door widened some more. 'Yes, that's me.' He strode forward, stepped out onto the top step. 'Are you from the police?'

I kept my eyes fixed on him, allowed a momentary silence to sit between us while I avoided a direct answer to his question. 'I think it might be best if we went inside.'

My practiced manner of officialdom seemed to have worked. He turned back towards the door, beckoned me inside. I noticed Mr Donald had bulked up with several layers of clothing, a scarf above his cardigan. He spoke, 'You'll have to excuse the temperature … boiler packed in.'

I nodded. 'I can handle a bit of cold.'

'Well, we're used to it, happens every year … hellish getting someone out, mind you.' He led me through to the kitchen, motioned me sit at a large pine table. 'Tea?'

I was tempted, but declined. Something stronger would have been closer to the mark.

As I lowered myself at a seat by the wall, the door to the kitchen opened once more. A small, frail woman in a long Arran jumper appeared. I could tell from the pictures I'd

seen of Kirsty that this was her mother; the resemblance
was striking.

I started to rise.

'No, don't get up,' she said.

'This is my wife, Sheila, and this is ...' Mr Donald
looked at me. 'Sorry, I don't think I caught your name.'

'My name's Doug Michie ... I'm an investigator, and
I'm looking into your recent loss.'

Sheila raised a hand to her shoulder, then another traced
the line of her arm. The mention of her daughter seemed to
be enough to unleash a torrent of grief.

I went on, 'I should say, I'm not police. I was once, but
this is a private affair.'

Sheila looked towards her husband. 'Frank ... I don't
understand.'

'Neither do I,' he said. 'I think you should explain
yourself.'

I laced my fingers before me on the table, lowered my
tone and tried to explain the reasons why I was looking into
the murder of their daughter. My reasons didn't seem to
matter, though; they had lost Kirsty and nothing I could say
or do would alter that fact.

'I don't know about this,' said Frank. He folded his arms
across his chest, a defensive posture.

Sheila moved towards the table, removed a chair. She
turned back to face her husband but her words seemed to be
directed towards me. 'I think we should hear him out, dear.
What harm can it do?'

Frank bridled, unfolded his arms and raised his palms
towards the ceiling. He turned away from us and leaned on
the sink, staring out the window into the back garden.

I went for broke. 'Maybe you can tell me a little bit
about your daughter?'

Sheila's eyes glassed over as she spoke about her

daughter: about her school days, her dance classes, her love for her job, all the promise she showed and all her parents' hopes.

I let her speak herself out; if nothing else, it seemed to calm Frank.

'You mentioned her job … '

'She worked for me,' said Frank.

I turned to face him. 'What did she do?'

'She minded the show home … I'm a builder. I put some flats up by the harbour.' He brushed at the stubble on his neck with the back of his fingers. 'She loved that job, couldn't get her away from the place.'

'Is that where she met … Glenn?'

Frank looked at his wife; she raised a hand to his. He nodded slowly, words too much of a trial for him.

I pressed. 'I take it you didn't get along with Glenn?'

Sheila seemed to be the one with strength now. 'Mr Michie, he's in custody for the murder of our daughter.'

I unlaced my fingers, leaned back in the chair and allowed myself a few seconds to compose my thoughts. 'I have to tell you both that in my experience an early arrest, like Glenn's, very rarely leads to a secure conviction.'

Frank dropped his wife's hand. 'What are you saying?'

I gulped down my words, let the pair adjust to the new atmosphere in the room. For a second, I thought I'd gone too far, then I saw Sheila's intelligence shining in her eyes. She spoke first. 'No. Let him finish, Frank.'

'Well, what are you trying to say?' he said.

It took all my courage to look Kirsty Donald's father in the eye as I spoke. 'I've seen cases like this in the past. I know how police forces work, and *don't* work. And I know a cover-up when I see one.'

Frank looked down at his wife. Her face was firm, hard. All the colour that sat in her cheeks earlier had left. I tried to draw my gaze away, to take in Frank's expression, but I knew he wasn't the one making the decisions here. Sheila reached out to her husband and grabbed him towards her; she laid her face on his hand for a moment and placed a delicate kiss on his fingertips. When she spoke this time she was looking at me, but speaking for every mother that had lost a child. 'We need to know the truth.'

Chapter 13

We'd had a week of on-off storms. The Scottish media had likened them to hurricanes, but then we'd always been good at bigging up our misfortunes. The pavements outside were criss-crossed with bits of broken tiles and slates blown from the roofs. A bus had been toppled. A fallen tree demolished a garage. YouTube was full of runaway trampolines and airborne wheelie bins. I couldn't see what all the fuss was about; we'd had bad weather before but there was something in the collective psyche now that demanded a short-term beat-up of anything vaguely new. I shook my head as I took my pint from the bar, tried to ignore the storm without: I had enough troubles of my own to worry about.

Smugglers was, for the main, empty. A few dole moles. A couple of bluenoses playing dominoes – making a racket every time they rattled the tray for a new game. The TV was playing; a bloke in beer-bottle glasses checked his luck at the ponies; the weather hadn't halted much then. It would truly be a national crisis if the footie was called off at the weekend. Somerset Boab would be doing a song about it.

I blew the froth off my pint of heavy and picked up the Ayrshire Post. The paper had changed a fair bit since my last stint in my old home town – it seemed to have grown up and turned into a real newspaper. I remembered wading through page after page of random punters holding onto big cheques. Of scouring the photos for a squint at an old face you once knew. Not now. There was proper news. I wondered if it was a sign of the times: had the Auld Toun developed into a place worthy of detailed press scrutiny? I found myself nodding sagely to myself. I knew the place I called home once again had changed. But, it wasn't only the papers doing the digging.

As the door to the main bar opened, a shower of rain splashed on the floor. The young girl in the parka stamped her feet and started to shiver. When she took her hood down her lips showed blue against her pale white face. She looked around, exchanged a nod with the barman and then registered the Post in my hands.

She took two steps towards me. 'Doug is it?'

I stood up, held out my hand, 'You must be Rachel Maciver.'

'You can just call me Rachel …'

I smiled, almost laughed at myself. 'Sorry, I've been reading your stories in the paper … the ones with the big by-line.'

She seemed to be thawing, pulled out a chair and ordered herself a half of Guinness. Rachel looked too young to be doing her job; nothing like the hacks they sent out to crime scenes I'd attended in Ulster.

'So, you're a friend of Glenn's mum,' she said.

I nodded. 'Old friend.'

She smiled. Some colour was returning to her lips. 'I didn't know him that well, only through Kirsty … she was my wee sister's friend. You know that though.'

I'd found Rachel on the list Lyn had given me; she seemed like a contact I could make some use of. 'Tell me a little bit about Kirsty.'

'Not Glenn? I thought it was Glenn you were trying to

get off.' I watched her pick up her half-Guinness and take a sip, wipe away a creamy layer from her top lip.

For a moment, I felt tested. Was she after a reaction? I held firm. 'I'm simply looking into the circumstances of her death.' I felt like I was watching my words; she was a journalist after all.

'Look, I'm not trying to be funny with you, Doug ... I don't think Glenn was capable of murder either.'

She seemed to have my mind made up for me. 'Either?'

She put her drink back on the table, ran the back of her hand over her mouth. 'Nobody does ... not anyone that knew him. Or Kirsty.'

'What do you mean?'

She lit up, leaned on the table and tapped a tattoo with a beer mat. 'I mean, they had their moments, their rows ... but murder! Get real.'

I wasn't sure where she was going with this, but she clearly had some kind of theory. I sat back in my chair, crossed my leg over. As I did so, I noticed an umbrella fly past the window; the sight distracted me, took my train of thought with it. Rachel traced the arc of my gaze with her own eyes.

'What are you saying? You don't believe the official version of events?' I said.

'Which is what? Kirsty had her first fit in years, brought on by a beating from Glenn ... No. I don't go for that.'

'Well, why haven't you said?'

She huffed. 'Eh, *hello* ... I think I just did.'

'I meant to the police.'

Rachel shook her head, made a moue of her mouth. 'Do I look mental?'

'You don't think they'd believe you?'

Her voice pitched. 'And like I'd be believed, Doug.' She scraped a fingernail along the table top as her voice continued to climb. 'You know, I might not have been a reporter all that long but I've seen enough of what goes on in this town to know that there's certain people you don't take on ...' She stopped herself, started to scan the room to see who had been listening.

'Like who?'

'Uh-uh ...' She clamped her mouth tight. She was practicing Rabbie's advice: *learn taciturnity and let that be your motto.* I couldn't fault her but neither did it help me.

'Rachel, if you have something I can use, you owe it to Kirsty and to Glenn to let me know.'

She took a long draft of her Guinness, wiped her mouth again and reached under the table for her bag. 'I'm not getting involved.'

'Rachel ...'

Her eyes flared. 'I can't do anything. I'm a cub reporter on a local rag ... not John Pilger.'

'I'm not asking you to take on the establishment, Rachel.'

That huff again. 'Oh, aren't you?'

She was talking in riddles. She was also rattled, that much I could see. I watched her zip up her parka, wrap her scarf round her neck and wrestle the strap of her bag over her shoulder. With each movement she made I knew I was edging dangerously close to losing the chance to get her to reveal what she knew. 'You can trust me, you know.'

My words seemed to trigger her sarcasm nerve; she tilted her head to the side. 'Weren't you *filth*?'

I felt my neck tighten. 'I was police.'

'Yeah, well ... you all stick together don't you?'

I stifled a laugh, but I couldn't hold back the sly smile. 'You're kidding, aren't you? They kicked me out.'

'And why was that?'

My eyes lolled in the back of my head. The reasons for

my departure were already droll to me. 'I guess they didn't like me very much.'

Rachel sat still, staring into my soul for a few seconds. Something was going on with her, not thinking exactly, or even allowing thoughts to form; she seemed to be intuiting. In an instant she opened her bag, thrust in her hand, and removed a blue folder. She held it in the air for a moment, her gaze fixed on mine. 'This isn't anything you couldn't find in the public domain – by spending a day Googling or getting inky fingers in the library. But that's not to say I don't think it's valuable.'

I stared at the file. 'What is it?'

She rose, slapped the file on the table as she turned for the door. 'It's interesting reading, that's what it is.'

I reached a hand out for the file. 'Hang on, I might have some questions.'

She put her hood up. 'I'm quite sure you will, Doug.'

Chapter 14

I didn't know why, but it seemed like the time for Tom Waites' *Rain Dogs*. I played the surreal *Cemetery Polka* as I pulled into my mother's driveway on the edge of Alloway. The sensory battering of recent days had started to take its toll. There was plenty I needed to process, think about, but somehow my priorities seemed to be drifting elsewhere. I removed my mobile phone from my pocket as the car's engine stilled. I wanted to check with my sister after my earlier call.

Ringing.

'C'mon, Claire ... pick up.'

More ringing.

Then the answer phone picked up my call.

'Hello, Claire ... it's Doug again, just checking you got my last message. I really think we need to have a chat about the old girl.' I toyed with the idea of hanging up, the moment passed. 'So, look, give me a call when you have a chance, eh?'

I hung up. I hoped I hadn't sounded too harsh; it was easy for someone like me – with no ties, no immediate family – to forget that Claire had a life of her own now. Could I judge her for not looking out for my mother? I doubted it.

The front door was open as I walked in; a familiar musty

smell greeted me. I turned, closed the door. I noticed condensation clinging to the windowpanes. I ran a desultory finger down the layer of moisture: the place was going to ruin. Maintenance had always been my father's job.

I called out, 'Hello … anybody home?'

No answer.

I walked the length of the hall to the kitchen. As I pushed the door there seemed to be something blocking the way. I eased back, heard a shuffle of old bones and knew Ben was lying in the way. I gave the dog a moment to right himself, tried the handle once more.

He greeted me with his tail wagging, 'Hello, boy …'

I reached down to pat his head, then I noticed the state of the kitchen. He'd relieved himself, defecated on the floor. By the looks of things he hadn't been out for days. He seemed to sense my discovery, slunk back from me, ears pinned down. The look of shame on the old dog's face was heartbreaking.

'It's all right, fella …' I took him by the collar to the back door, led him out to the garden. He lolled down the steps and released his bladder, his arthritic legs shaking as he tried to hold himself up.

'God Almighty …' I looked back indoors. 'What have you been playing at woman?'

I left Ben to sniff around the lawn's edges. The sight of him dug at me; reminded me of an old reel I'd seen of pit ponies being led out to grass for the first time in their sorry lives. I turned for the door.

'Mam … Mam … Where are you?'

I stood still, waited for a reply but none came. My first reaction had been anger; hurt at the sight of the dog and the house, but now I was struck by worry. Where was she? What had happened?

I raced through to the living room: empty. I turned for

the dining room, likewise no-one in sight. I bolted up the stairs and knocked on my mother's bedroom door. There was no reply. I battered louder, called out: 'Mam! Mam!'

Silence.

I turned the handle and went inside. A thick foetid air greeted me. The bed hadn't been made, probably hadn't been touched in days, weeks maybe. The curtains were shut tight, blocking out the daylight. I moved towards the window, flooded the room with light. Dust particles danced. I flipped the latch and let the breeze come inside. I stood staring at the carnage of a life in ruins. The room was a mess. Dinner plates piled by the bed. Chocolate bar wrappers on the floor. Empty bottles. Was this really the way my mother was living?

I kicked out at the mattress, walked back through the door. In the hallway I stood for a moment wondering what had gone on, where she could be. For a second I felt defeated, I rushed into the spare room; it was empty. Then I made for my sister's room. My late father had turned it into a study. A place to go and pretend to read, follow his few interests; in reality, it was a place to nap and hide from the world.

Something stirred in the corner of the room as I entered. At once I recognised the huddle of bones on the floor.

'Mam ... what the?'

I leant over, touched the sleeve of her dressing gown. She stirred some more, muttered. The smell of drink was thick in the air. I tried to get her upright; she was almost lifeless in my arms. As I sat her against the wall a bottle of Grouse was evacuated from the folds of her gown. It rolled away from us, barely a drop of liquid swilling in the bottle's base. I lashed out with the heel of my shoe, knocked the bottle to the other side of the room.

My mother was drunk as twelve monkeys. I realised at

once I'd have to get her walking, talking. I needed to pour some coffee into her. 'Come on, Mam, let's get you on your feet.'

A groan. 'What … What's going on?'

'We're going to get you up and about.' I raised her; her head lolled from side to side. Her face looked pale, almost grey. I'd heard the expression *close to the grave* before but I'd never actually witnessed it in a loved one at such close quarters. The sight of my mother provoked shame in me, deep shame for what she'd become. But, also, I felt a new responsibility grip me: this was the woman who had raised me; now the world had turned and I was going to be the one who had to look after her.

My mother seemed suddenly electrified with an energy, a rage: 'What the hell's going on?'

'Mam, we're going to get some coffee into you.'

'I don't want coffee!'

I had to struggle to keep my grip on her. She pushed me away. Her strength surprised me. Her frame was so thin, wiry. 'Mam, now c'mon …'

She cursed at me. I loosed my grip on her. 'Just leave me. Leave me. Get out of my house.'

I watched her press her shoulder to the wall, manage two or three steps before she slumped against the plaster and let herself slide onto the carpet once more. She curled over and seemed to pass instantly into deep, heavy sleep. I picked her up, she was so light. Nothing of her, that's what people would say. I returned her to her bed. I pulled the duvet over and made sure she was comfortable, sound. She looked lost to the world. Deep in dreams. I wondered what they were about.

For a moment I stood, just watching, but the sight was too painful. I moved away, closed the window a little, drew the curtains and placed a glass of water by the bedside.

I left her to sleep it off.

Downstairs, I brought the dog in. Cleaned up the mess in the kitchen. I was opening a new packet of Marlboro, sparking up, when my phone started to ring in my pocket.

It was Claire. The sight of her name in the caller ID made my pulse race with anger. I knew she wasn't to blame, but I knew that's how siblings operated. The weight of family grief was a load to be shared.

'You got my message.' I was brusque.

'I did, yeah …'

There didn't seem any point in pleasantries now. 'Then maybe you can tell me what the hell is going on with our mother?'

Chapter 15

There didn't seem any point in keeping things from her. At least, that's what I'd decided at this moment. I knew, full well, that I might feel differently after revealing what I'd uncovered. I waited for Lyn in the drawing room of my Queens Terrace guest house with a shot of Talisker in hand, the ice clinking every so often on the side of the glass. It was too cold for the ice to thaw. I didn't mind, it kept an edge on the whisky.

The radio seemed to be stuck on WestFM, playing some Human League from the 1980s. I felt strangely transported back to more innocent times; could see the blonde girl singing about working as a waitress in a cocktail bar. Music was so much better then. Maybe it was just because it was my music. My era. My youth. It seemed to have more heart. Everything looked too slick, too manufactured to me now.

Lyn appeared, seemed to tap into my reverie. 'Don't you want me, baby?'

I smiled. 'They don't write them like that anymore.'

Lyn took the strap from her shoulder, placed her bag on the ground next to her chair. 'Oh come on, it wasn't all great.'

'Two words: Ultravox, Vienna.'

A laugh. She tipped her head back. 'Kept off number

one by *Shaddap You Face*, I seem to remember.'

She had me. 'I think that's check-mate.'

A smile. She raised a finger in the air, hissed through her teeth. 'No kidding it is.'

I got out of my seat, went to the bar to collect a drink for Lyn. Diet Coke and ice – the ice crackled as it hit the fizzy liquid. My landlady, Mrs Kerr, still upright in her tabard, drew me a look as I passed over the cash. 'What?' I said.

'New lady friend, is it?'

I tilted my head, twisted down the corner of my mouth. 'Please ...'

A blatant change of subject. 'Will you be joining us for dinner this evening, Mr Michie?'

'I don't think so ... not this evening.'

Then, back on track. 'Oh, dining out are we?' A smile. Eyes over my shoulder towards Lyn. 'With erm ...'

I took my change, turned away. 'Thank you.'

Lyn was tapping her foot to a new track on the radio as I arrived. It seemed a shame to break her groove, but I needed privacy. 'Look, would you mind if we took these upstairs?'

She lapsed into mock indignation. 'Douglas Michie ... what kind of girl do you take me for?'

I held out my hand. 'My kind.'

'Well, in that case.'

As we left the drawing room, Mrs Kerr maintained her posture at the bar, glancing insouciantly as we passed. I thought to myself: you're as well hung for a sheep as a lamb.

Lyn managed a laugh at the picture on my bedroom wall. 'Oh, my God ... I never thought I'd see that again.'

'Oh yeah, the Lassie dog.'

She giggled again, touched the side of her mouth. 'This place is in a time warp.' She turned to face me. 'Do they have the green lady picture … and those Spanish orphan kids anywhere?'

I shook my head. 'Erm, no.'

'Are you sure?'

'Well, I haven't seen them.'

'Maybe you should take a look.'

I pulled out the only chair, motioned Lyn to sit. 'I've had better things to do.'

She took the hint, lowered herself in the creaking upholstery and started to sip at her Diet Coke. For a moment, she looked almost guilt-ridden. It was as if she had suddenly recalled the fate Glenn faced and her recent levity felled her. 'Well, you better tell me what you've been doing.'

I knew she wouldn't like to hear it, but I had to come clean. After all, I never said I wasn't going to see Kirsty's parents. 'I visited the Donalds.'

'Oh …'

I had expected more of a reaction. 'They're good people.'

Nodded. 'I told you that.'

'They don't hate Glenn, you know …'

Her eyes stared out to sea. 'No?'

I laid it out for her. Relayed the highlights of my visit, what we'd discussed. How they appeared. 'I think they had their doubts about Glenn. I mean, they had pretty high expectations for Kirsty, and Glenn …'

'Was hardly marriage material.'

I held my words in check. Changed tack. 'I think I convinced them that there could be more to their daughter's death than the police are letting on.'

Lyn returned her gaze to me. Her brow tightened. 'What do you mean?'

I took a sip of my Talisker, lowered the glass. The ice crackled a little. 'The other night, I followed up on a hunch and let's just say it brought some focus to the investigation.'

She twisted in her seat, leaned forward. 'Go on.'

'I spoke to a contact I have on the force. I can't tell you what he said because that would place you and him in danger if it ever got out. But I think I'm onto something.'

Lyn put down her glass, stood up. She was inches from me as she spoke. 'Onto what?'

I looked away. I didn't know how wise it was to let her know what I knew.

Lyn reached out, grabbed my arm. 'Onto what, Doug?'

Our eyes locked. 'I was given a file.'

'A file, what kind of file?'

'A dossier ... it was compiled by someone who'd been looking into some unusual goings on down at the Port of Ayr.'

Lyn scrunched her 'brows. 'I don't understand.'

'I didn't either, at first, but I looked through the file and I spotted a face that I recognised.'

'Who?'

She started to shiver before me. I held her hands in mine. 'It doesn't matter who. If the pieces of the puzzle click into place you'll find out in good time. There'll be no way of keeping it quiet ... right now, the less you know the better.'

'But, I need to know, Doug. They have my son, I need to know ...'

I tightened my grip. 'Lyn, if I'm right, this runs deep. Trust me, I have to keep you in the dark, for your own safety.'

'Oh, Doug ...' She buried her head in my chest. 'I'm not strong enough for this.'

I placed my fingers beneath her chin, raised her face. 'Hey, you're plenty strong enough. I know you of old, remember?'

She smiled, a small smile that suddenly gave way to an uninhibited heartmelter. I didn't know why, or how, but my reassurance had done the trick. I could tell Lyn believed in me as our eyes met and locked again. She quickly pressed her lips onto mine and the fiery sting of Talisker was reignited once more.

Chapter 16

The chips and curry sauce from the Harbour Views Chinese had solidified in the container by the time I got round to opening it. I'd bought them without really possessing a proper appetite. I had a hunger, but it wasn't for food. The streets of Auld Ayr seemed to be closing in on me as I shuffled into the wind that wailed down Fort Street. By the Academy I was nearly bent double. The thought of tackling food deserted me and I loped towards the nearest bin to dump what should have been my comfort food. Any comfort was in short supply. My mind was racing with thoughts of Lyn, the case, and just what I had got myself into.

At the edge of Cathcart Street I sheltered in the lee of a building I once knew but now only confused me. I looked up and down: it seemed to have been converted into flats. The last time I'd seen it, the place was a tea room; a pleasant enough place called The Apple Tree. They sold scones and jam there; Glasgow Fair punters came doon the water for their fish tea. It reeked of tradition, but there didn't seem to be any place in the town for tradition anymore.

I turned my face towards the Sandgate as a host of shrieks assailed the airwaves. Young girls, their party dresses pitched higher than their voices. I shook my head as I watched them go; the sight of their bare legs made me feel colder; I knew I was getting old. I felt parental, even though I had no children of my own. Something deep inside me said the group shouldn't be out on their own like that. Was it the case again? Was it the thought of Kirsty Donald's real killer being on the loose? Or was it a wider protective sense I felt towards the town of my birth? I wondered about many things.

Ayr had changed beyond any possibility I would have entertained only a short time ago; I wanted the old place back, the familiar, the secure. I didn't like what I'd learned about the Auld Toun since my return. I dug into my pocket and removed a packet of Marlboro. I had started smoking the red-tops again, abandoned my usual brand because the local version couldn't be relied upon with all the bootlegging in the town. I found I quite liked the taste of the Marlboro once more. It was at the force's training academy in Tulliallan that I had last smoked the red-tops; my sergeant didn't like the smell, called them 'funny fags' and so I grew away from them. I smiled at the memory: it was all conditioning; that's what the force had really been about. I'd been taught that my own opinions, my own instincts and assumptions, my tastes, were worthless. There was a bigger picture, a wider understanding that I had no right to question.

I drew on the Marlboro, blew a thin trail of smoke into the darkness of the night sky. I knew Mason was encountering resistance in the force; the high heid yins didn't like having their authority tested. There was a course called the path of least resistance and smart coppers knew to stick to it. I knew that had been my problem – I never fitted the mould of a smart copper. That type, they rose in the ranks and ascended the K-ladder. They made friends and they kept them. In time, their friends kept them. It was a tried and tested formula; even had their own wee club with its own wee traditions to play up to.

I allowed myself a smile at the thought. I knew I stuck out from the boys in the Craft.

'Daft laddie.' I heard myself say the words. They weren't mine, well, not originally. They'd been those of a DC I'd been buddied with at the outset of my career.

'You're nothing but a daft laddie, Doug,' Billy Morrison had said when I told him I was taking the RUC job. 'You could have been set up for life here ... all you had to do was keep your head down.'

I was never any good at that. The memory was as clear as Technicolor to me now. I'd well and truly strayed from the path of least resistance.

I took another draw on the filter tip and headed off Cathcart Street, back towards the old school. At Dansarena I dowped my cigarette on the wall and pulled up my collar. The road back to the guest house was dark, the night cold, and my thoughts edging into ratiocination. I needed to relax, unwind and let my aching head find some form of distraction. Football. Car-crash television. It didn't matter to me.

On Citadel Place I started to become dimly aware of footsteps behind me; heavy footsteps. I turned, looked back up the road I'd travelled but the footsteps stopped and in the darkness it was hard to trace more than the outline of car-roofs beneath the direct sheen of the street-lamps. I halted, wondered if I'd imagined the noise and returned to the path – but with a hurried gait. It'd managed a dozen or so steps when I heard the footfalls again, this time they were running. As I turned, I suddenly grasped for breath: I doubled over with a fist in my gut. I lunged, felt another fist in my kidney and then I fell to the ground in a hail of sharp, fast punches. The fists moved quickly, were joined by dark, heavy boots that connected soundly with my ribs and my stomach and my chest.

I felt blood rise in my mouth. I spat out a mouthful. Tried to make a sound but was unable. I was outnumbered and, I suspected, outclassed. The pair were not even drawing heavy breath when they halted.

I was rolled onto my back. I raised my hands to shield my face in a defensive movement.

'Get his arms.' The voice was loud, certain. It carried the authority of someone who was used to giving orders.

I managed a low blow, kicked out and caught the smaller of the two in the groin.

'The arms, get his arms behind his back,' came again.

I recognised the manoeuvre: they were preparing for a cuffing. Probably on instinct.

As my arms were locked the larger of the two assailants came into view, his face obscured by a balaclava. He grabbed my cheeks in his hand. I noticed the gold ring on his finger as he spoke. 'Right, Michie, you'll only get this warning once, so you better take it or the next step for you is off the brig.' He squeezed tighter. I could see the jagged tips of his grey teeth. 'Stay away from what doesn't concern you . . .'

I found a line of ferocity. 'And what would that be?'

My arms were twisted tighter. 'Want me to panel him?' said the voice behind me.

The balaclava spoke again; he seemed to be smiling. 'Oh, you are that stupid, eh . . . The Donald lassie isn't your concern, Michie. Stay away, stay well away.'

As he leaned back he raised his boot off the ground. His heavy sole was the last thing I saw before it connected with my forehead and the night went from darkness to blackness.

Chapter 17

The brightness of the hospital ward struck me like another assault. I opened my eyes only briefly, but long enough to take in the full glare of industrial lighting and white walls beyond white bed sheets. I scrunched my 'brows, tightened my eyelids. Nothing seemed to block out the glare. Then the pain kicked in. Shooting pain, around my eye-sockets and clean across the top of my head. I felt like a bandsaw was being operated on my skull. On instinct, I tried to lift a hand to my face; at once, I knew my arm was too heavy. I ventured another squint into the room to confirm my suspicions. I was right, my arm was in plaster.

I let out an elongated sigh. My head swam as I leaned back into the pile of pillows behind me; it was enough to alert the nurse.

'Mr Michie,' she said. 'I wouldn't be making too many drastic movements.'

I tried to speak; my mouth had dried out. The words failed me.

'Here, take a sip of water,' said the nurse. Her voice was harsh, fully Ayrshire. A west-coast battler in a white apron. If I was hoping for bedside manner, I was going to be disappointed.

'What the hell happened?' I said.

'I was hoping you could tell me.' I still had my eyes held tightly shut, but I could hear the scorn in her voice. There was a time when this sort of thing might have bothered me, but another line of Rabbie's had sunk in by now: *let them cant about decorum*. I knew she thought I was another rowdy – someone who settled his problems with his fists. As I felt the stookie on my arm I knew that wasn't going to be an option for some time.

'I mean, how did I get here?'

She started to fiddle with the chart on the end of the bed, shuffled a few papers on the clipboard as she answered me. 'A member of the public brought you in ... well, called the ambulance to be more precise.' The clipboard rattled on the end of the bed. 'Look, don't be concerning yourself with that right now. You need to rest.'

I'd managed to adjust my eyes to the glare of the lights. I was still smarting but able to take her in. She had a face just how I imagined it: like a burst couch. 'You make that sound like an order, sister.' I put some sting in her title.

She placed her hands on her hips; they were broad hips. 'You better believe it. Sit tight, the doctor will be around to see you in a wee bit.' She strutted for the door.

When she was gone I raised myself in the bed, surveyed the damage that had been done from my thoroughly professional kicking. I felt bashed up inside: but it would take more than a bit of a street-mugging to put me off my stride. My main concern was the broken hand; that was personal. It was a reminder that the Devil found work for idle hands. That I was messing with the big boys.

I was holding up my plaster cast, trying to wriggle my bruised fingers when I spotted a broad figure blocking the doorway to the ward. It was Mason. I nodded towards him, and he started to make his way towards my bedside with his slow, slouching gait.

'Quite the picture, Doug,' he said. His expression held firm. His gaze looked guilty though; he couldn't meet my eyes.

I huffed. 'Is this an official police visit?'

He drew closer to the bed, unbuttoned his jacket and removed a chair. 'No, I heard you'd had an accident –'

'Accident. Are you joking? I was properly worked over and you know that.'

'Look, Doug ...'

I raised my stookie. 'You see this? This is a personal message and I know who it's from, so don't be dancing round the houses with me, pal.'

The word pal seemed to unsettle him. 'I know. I know ... I'm sorry.'

'If I thought you had anything to apologise for, Mason, you wouldn't be wearing a sorry expression ... you'd be wearing your backside as a hat!'

He looked away. We both knew what the score was. There was no place for words here. We let the silence come between us, calm our nerves.

'I brought you something.' Mason reached into his coat.

'It better not be grapes.'

He placed a bottle of Talisker on the bedside table. I smiled. 'You better put that in the drawer. The sister runs a tight ship.'

He nodded, picked up the bottle and squirreled it away. 'How you feeling anyway?'

'Like I've been done in and had my hand broken.' Mason looked away, took in the sleeping patient in the next bed. I wondered if he was sussing out whether he could speak but the moment seemed to pass. I prompted, 'They were police, you know.'

'*What?*'

'Oh, come off it ...'

'Doug, I didn't know anything about this. I swear it.'

I tried to scratch beneath my plaster cast; my hand had started to itch. 'One of them had a very interesting gold ring. I got a good look at it, close enough to see the wee square and compasses ... they were from the Craft.'

Mason leaned back, raised palms. 'Now c'mon, doesn't mean they were polis!'

'One of them was for cuffing my arms behind my back ... do you think I'm stupid, Mason?'

He looked to the left, leaned forward on his seat and lowered his voice. 'Well, I swear to you ... if I'd known, Doug.'

He knew now. I replayed his warning to me in Belleisle: he didn't want to get involved. Was he scared? I doubted it. Mason was a rock. He took threats in the same way as me: like incitement. If he was wary it was because he had more information to tell me and he knew what I'd do with it. Mason liked to keep a low profile; he'd stayed home in Ayr, tried to play the game. But that didn't mean he liked the rules anymore than I did.

I went for broke. 'You've reached the end of the road, mate.'

His eyes widened. 'What do you mean?'

'How long have I known you?'

'Oh, Jesus, the old-pals act again, eh?'

'No. What I'm saying is, I know you. And I've never seen you this rattled.'

He lowered his head, shook it from left to right as he stared at the floor tiles. 'It's all a mess.'

I reached out my broken hand, placed it on his shoulder. 'Well, let's clean it up.'

Chapter 18

I'd read about amputees who still felt fingers and limbs itch from time to time. As I stood with my injured hand raised to my eyes I longed for some relief from what felt like an ant infestation below the plaster cast. The itching had started the second I left the hospital and hadn't let up. I shook my head, tried to turn my thoughts towards other things. It was a trial, but I just about managed it as the bus pulled up and I stepped on. The road back to Ayr was wet, pot-hole scarred, and the bus full of disgruntled, weather-weary punters. The windows steamed as the moisture rose from coats and hats. I wiped a porthole in the condensation with the sleeve of my uninjured arm and stared out at the dreich Ayrshire fields.

'Cheer up, son. Och, you've never died a winter yet!' It was an old woman in a raincoat, wispy-white hair hung beneath a woollen beret she wore at too jaunty an angle. She looked like an escapee from The Muppets.

I smiled, tried not to encourage her. I knew the type; if I engaged her I'd be forced to endure yakking about the grandweans or the price of fish. I couldn't face it. I turned back to the window and my gloom. I was watching the litter blowing by as my mobile phone started to ring.

'Hello …'

'So, you're going ahead with this then?' It was Lyn.

'I don't see what choice I've got.'

Her voice climbed. 'You could follow the doctor's orders and stay in hospital.'

I didn't want to go through this again – I had fended off Lyn's insistence that I stay in the ward once already. 'We've been through this … I'm fine.'

'Doug, you have a broken hand and a head injury.'

I felt the bus hit another pot-hole. I jolted in my seat. 'Look, I have things to do. You know that.'

'It can wait.'

I felt my chest tighten, impatience biting. 'No, Lyn, it can't. Who's going to tackle this if I stay in hospital?'

'But …'

'No buts. That's what they want, Lyn … me in hiding. The whole idea was to scare me off. There's a plan in place for your son to take a fall and I don't see anyone else doing a thing about it.' When I stopped ranting I realised how harsh I must have sounded, 'I'm sorry. I don't mean to lecture you, but this is the way it has to be.'

Lyn spoke. 'I just don't want you to get hurt.'

I looked at my hand in plaster, shook my head. I knew it was too late for that. I also knew the next step was much worse than a broken hand. 'Don't you worry about me, Lyn.'

'But, I do.'

I felt a pulse in my temple start to accelerate, 'I have to go, Lyn. We'll speak soon.'

I heard her say goodbye and I hung up.

When I stepped off the bus I took a walk towards Burns Statue Square. The top of the town was faring so much better than the other end. The Ayrshire and Galloway seemed to be doing good trade but the old Hong Kong was gone, replaced by a trendier-looking joint. I remembered when it was The Statue Bar as well. On instinct I found myself looking over to see how The Hussar was these days. It was gone. The building boarded up. I felt a sadness at the passing into obscurity of another part of my youth; I'd had good times there, once. All watched over by the wry eye of Rabbie up on his plinth. My head started to fill with the myriad quotes I'd stored from Burns. So much of it had seeped into me, but at this moment only one gem stuck: *a man's a man for aw that.*

I crossed the road at Killoch Place and headed up the Square to the train station. Outside Wallace's I was stopped by a skanky-looking youth in joggies and a Rangers vest. It was freezing out and he shivered uncontrollably as he stuck his hand out. 'Got a pound-fifty for me, pal?'

I stopped dead in my tracks. 'You'd be better with a square meal, son.' His eyes glossed over. He went into a spiel about needing bus-fare to visit his sick daughter. He didn't look much older than a child himself. I made no reply, had heard it a million times before. But not in Ayr; the junkie-tide had obviously risen. I put the bead on him, and he staggered off to try another passer-by.

The black cabs were stretched all the way down to Kyle Street; I wondered how it was possible for so many of them to make a living in the Auld Toun. I stepped into the first on the rank and caught the driver eyeing my stookie with disdain. He obviously thought I was a rowdy, was worried I'd kick off in his cab. I tried a smile on him as I gave my destination: 'The port office.'

He tapped it into the TomTom and said, 'Oh, yeah, I know where that is.' His accent was London, prime Cockney. The SatNav made sense.

On the way down to the harbour my hand continued to itch as the driver treated me to a discourse on what was wrong with Tottenham Hotspur, peppering his chat with fond reminiscences of Ricky Villa and Steve Archibald.

I tried not to look when he got teary-eyed about Glenn Hoddle. At the port offices I paid up and felt my stomach turn as I was given a 'Cheers, Gov.' I imagined the cabbie singing *Chat, Chat, Rabbit, Rabbit* on the way back to the Smith Street rank.

The wind battered the coast and blew up to the Port of Ayr's Arran Terminal. Two large hydraulic cranes tackled some recently unloaded scrap, the noise of metal on metal shrieking straight into my bones. I felt a shiver pass through me for what I was about to do. I had given the move very little thought, mainly for fear of resiling from my plan. Since my dead-of-night encounter with Ayrshire's finest, however, the stakes had risen. It was time to rattle some cages. If I ended up at the bottom of the water, weighed down with some of that hefty scrap metal, then that was the risk I was going to have to take.

I pulled the door towards me. The wind caught it and the rusty hinges sung. I saw a young girl sitting behind a white-to-grey counter. She raised her head as I wrestled the door closed with one hand and approached her.

My first instinct was to dispense with pleasantries, but manners got the better of me. 'Bit blowy out,' I said.

She didn't look used to seeing too many people lob up at her counter. 'Is there something I can help you with?' Her voice was cold.

I smiled. The show of teeth failed to thaw her. 'I'd like to see Mr Crawford, please.'

She tilted her head on her neck. 'Do you have an appointment with the Councillor?'

She obviously liked his official title; I didn't see what use it was here though. I put away my teeth. 'No. But I do have this.' I clanked my plaster cast down on the counter. In my fingers was a picture I'd printed of the councillor with Jonny Gilmour outside the Davis Snooker Club. 'I'm sure that'll be enough to get his interest, if you'd like to pass it along.'

Chapter 19

The receptionist was called Jennifer. I knew that because as she took my request for a meeting through to Councillor Crawford I was left staring at her name-tag on the counter. She'd also left the appointments diary, which I picked up and skimmed through. Most of the entries were uninteresting, names of reps and repair men. The odd delivery details. But as I trawled the entries I spotted a name which caused my eyes to widen.

'By the holly …'

It had been nothing more than suspicion up until now, but there it was in black and white. Kirsty Donald had made an appointment with the Port Authority the day before she died. I flicked further back in the diary and there she was again. Writ large. I felt my pulse quicken as I returned the diary to the counter and stepped back.

I was drawing deep breaths, trying to cool my jets as Jennifer appeared again. She had left holding my photograph of the Councillor and Jonny Gilmour, but her hands were now empty.

'Councillor Crawford would like to see you in his office, Mr Michie …' she took two steps to the front, turned briskly towards another door and opened it up. 'This way, please.'

The door led to a thinly carpeted hallway. Grey industrial-looking walls skirted the well-worn floor. I saw a door towards the end of the walkway and figured now was going to be my only chance to approach Jennifer with a query.

'You must have an idea why I'm here,' I said.

She turned; her mouth drooped for a moment. 'I'm sorry?'

'I'm investigating the death of Kirsty Donald. You knew her didn't you?'

Jennifer's heavy eyelids fluttered in double-quick time. She was rattled. I knew she had been warned off right away. 'I'm just a receptionist ...'

'I know she came here the day before she died, Jennifer.'

The girl looked away. We'd reached the door to Crawford's office. She leaned towards me, dropped her voice. 'Look, I only work here ... I don't know anything.'

I watched the young girl reach out for the door handle. As she gripped it I could see her eyes moistening. 'Think about what you're saying, Jennifer ... we're dealing with murder here. You do realise that.'

Her cheeks suddenly flushed, she pushed the door open and stepped away.

Councillor Crawford was sitting behind his desk, staring at a computer screen. He affected to be engrossed in little rows and columns of numbers for a moment and then removed his thick glasses and rose to greet me.

'Ah, Mr Michie ...' He turned to the receptionist. 'Thank you Jennifer, that will be all.'

On the desk between us sat the picture I'd used as my calling card. I could see the face of Jonny Gilmour clearly. The Councillor was just as easily identifiable in the glare of the lights from the Davis Snooker Club. I walked over and tapped my plaster cast down on the desk. The photograph jumped.

'You seem to have attained a nasty injury, Mr Michie.'

I smiled. 'Very nasty. In fact I'd say the way I *attained* this injury couldn't have been nastier.'

'Oh ...'

I positioned myself on the edge of his desk, just high enough to peer down my nose at him. I liked the vantage point it afforded me. 'We won't go into that now, Councillor ... I'm here to talk about more pressing matters.' I picked up the photograph. 'Like your friendship with Jonny Gilmour.'

He leaned back in his seat. 'I don't see what that has to do with you.'

'I'm investigating the murder of Kirsty Donald, but I'm sure you're well aware of that by now.'

He held firm, not a flicker in his grey eyes.

I continued, 'You see, in the course of the investigation I've uncovered some very interesting facts, Councillor. Not just about the company you keep, although that in itself is very interesting.'

He shrugged, brought his bulk forward in his chair and laced his fingers over his belly. 'I'm not sure of the relevance of any of this –'

'Oh, no? Well, it seems to me that in the last few months there's been some quite interesting goings on down at the Port.'

He unhooked his hands, weighed the air with them. 'I'm lost.'

'Oh, come on now, don't play dumb.' I drew up the contents of the folder the Ayrshire Post reporter had given me. 'I'm talking about the gang arrests. The illegal immigrants that turned up in the ship's hold. The drugs haul. The smuggled vodka, oh and the ciggies, enough ciggies to sink a battleship ... Do I go on? Do I even mention the cannabis plants and the hydroponics kit?'

He put his hands flat on the desk and pushed himself up.

'You're talking about criminal acts. And, for that you need to see the police, Mr Michie.' He walked towards the door. I felt the swish of his brisk movements as he passed me. 'I'd like you to leave now.'

I eased myself off the edge of the desk. 'Are you seriously suggesting I take this to the police?'

He looked down at the floor. 'If you have concerns you should take them to the proper authorities.'

I laughed out loud, raised my plaster cast. 'This is how the police deal with my concerns, Councillor.'

His mouth twitched; he glanced at the door. A few beads of moisture had formed on his upper lip. He was losing patience with me. 'Then perhaps you'd be better keeping your concerns to yourself.'

I leaned forward and placed a heavy hand on the Councillor's shoulder. 'I wouldn't count on that as a strategy, mate." I grinned, a wide one. "You see, I have some very definite ideas about what's been going on down here and I'm not alone.'

'What do you mean by that?' He'd lost his steel.

'I mean, you should pick your friends more carefully, Councillor.' I tapped my stookie off his buttonhole as I left. He winced, then grimaced as I grabbed the door handle and closed it firmly behind me.

In the corridor I felt my 'brows moisten. I knew the phrase I was looking for was *setting the cat amongst the pigeons* but I'd have to wait and see if the strategy worked.

Jennifer was sitting behind the counter as I reached the reception area once more. I walked towards her and took a pen from the stand on the counter. I wrote my mobile number on the blotter. 'When your conscience returns, give me a call.'

Chapter 20

By the time I made my way back to the guest house on Queens Terrace the early evening light was on the wane. Orange street lamps had started to fizz overhead, illuminating a landing-strip that led all the way to the County Buildings. I watched a mother and toddler struggling along the street in a hurry to beat the downpour the dark sky threatened. I wouldn't be stopping out tonight. I'd prepared for the occasion with a full bottle of Talisker and some Marlboro red-tops. A part of me wanted to rebel, to warn me of my advancing years and pull tight on the reins of responsibility. But sometimes the self-destruct switch had to be flipped and now was one of those times.

Mrs Kerr was re-arranging umbrellas in the coat-stand by the hallway as I entered the guest house. Her gaze seemed to alight on my plaster cast before it even came into view. She threw her hands up to her mouth and spoke through her long, thin fingers. 'Oh, my word ... what in the name of the wee man has happened to you?'

'Just a bump.'

She raised her head as I spoke, took in the bruising that was coming out on my face. 'Just a bump ... what from, a steamroller?'

I tried a sneer. 'Something like that.'

Mrs Kerr walked towards me and placed her cold palms on my cheeks. 'Oh, you poor dear.' She shook her head. 'You should get up them stairs and into bed … I'll bring your tea up tonight.'

I had all the nourishment I needed in my carrier bag. 'Eh, thanks, but I've already eaten. Had a very heavy lunch. Think I might just try and get my head down for a bit. Maybe grab some telly.'

She removed her hands from my face, placed them in the pockets of her tabard. She seemed lost for words as I squeezed passed her, gripping the off-licence carrier tight to my chest.

My room was freezing, so I kept my coat on. As I closed the curtains I watched the thin material catch the draft from the sash window and float inwards. I bent down towards the foot of the radiator and turned the nozzle. Tried to tempt some heat into the room. I knew it was a losing battle as the familiar drip, drip started from within the radiator. It would take an hour to reach the neighbourhood of tepid. I leant over for the heavily scratched glass by the sink and unscrewed the cap on my bottle of whisky.

The first shot burned a warm glow down the middle of my chest; I felt immediately at home. As I refilled, the cold of the room quickly became an irrelevance. The time-worn furnishings and the musty air were nothing but a backcloth to the main event: whisky oblivion.

When my wife left, it was whisky that extended a warm hand. In Ulster, when I was shown the door, it was whisky that welcomed me back to the land of the living. And now, with a plaster cast in tow and a buckled head it was my old friend I turned to once again.

I thought of my mother, my repulsion at the state of the house, of the poor dog, and her: sodden drunk and lying comatose on the floor.

'Who are you to judge, Doug?' I mouthed towards the glass. 'Who indeed ...'

I had bawled out my sister over the state of my drunken mother, and been asked in return who the hell I thought I was talking to. Claire's words rung in my ears now: 'Where were you when Dad died and I had to put her back together?'

'You know I was in Ulster ... I couldn't leave the job,' I'd replied, pathetically.

'The job. That's all I ever heard from you, Doug ... and tell me, where's the precious job now?'

I didn't have an answer. Claire's words seared into my solar plexus, knocked me back worse than any blows.

She wasn't finished. 'And what makes you think you have a right to come home now, after all these years, and start dictating how we live our lives?'

'Claire, I was worried about her ... the place was a mess, the dog wasn't getting out ... I – I –'

'Shut up, Doug. This is all too little, too late ... where was this concern when she needed it? Where were you when we needed you?'

My reply was beyond weak. 'I was in ... Ulster.'

Claire seized on that. 'I live in Inverness. That's a four-hour drive, but I did it every week after Dad died. I was there for her. I pulled her through but I can't be there 24/7. I have a husband and children.' She started to get tearful. I realised now how unfair I'd been. 'I can't do everything, Doug, I can't ...'

The line died.

I could still hear her tear-filled voice, the pain and the hurt, but also the anger. She resented me. I'd let her down, hadn't held up my end of the load after our father died and I saw that now. But I still knew it was all about the job. I had put the job first many a time, every time. It cost me my wife, and my family. My health had been ransacked, and in the end, what had it meant to the RUC? Nothing. I thought I was doing good, keeping the streets safe. But I was wrong. I was merely an instrument that in the end outlived its usefulness. The people with their hands on the levers of Ulster didn't need, or want, me messing with their machinery.

I jumped with a start at a loud knock on the door. I hadn't realised the time. I was sitting in darkness, the glass in my hand empty. My back ached as I rose from the chair to address more banging on the door.

'I'm coming.' I could hear my words slurring.

I reached the wall, turned the light switch. My eyeballs retreated from the glare. I scrunched my lids tight again. 'Oh, man ...'

'Doug ... You okay in there?'

I recognised the voice. 'Yeah, coming.'

As I turned the handle on the door, Mason pushed through. He walked into the middle of the room. His girth seemed to fill the place. 'What were you doing? I was banging on that door for ages.'

My eyes hurt as I turned into the room; my knees loosened on the few steps towards the bed. I spotted Mason picking up the bottle of Talisker, tipping the open neck up. 'Have you tanned the whole bottle?'

I shrugged. My backbone felt like it had been removed and replaced with packing foam.

'All right,' said Mason. He headed towards the door. 'I'll try and get you some coffee. Because, my friend, we have some very serious stuff to talk about.'

Chapter 21

We took Mason's car because I was in no fit state to drive. As I sat in the front passenger's seat I felt uneasy, the glare of the lights above the road piercing into my eyes. I gouged my knuckles into my head in an effort to stop the hammering that was going on there but it made no difference. One day I'd realise that there was no release in drink, just a temporary fleeing sensation. When that started to wear off, you paid. Big time.

'Where are you taking us?' I called out to Mason.

'To try and sober you up ...'

'Is there nowhere closer?' I pointed to a signpost, 'We'll be in Kilmarnock next.'

Mason turned an eye on me, glowered. 'There's a Little Chef up here. They open late and I can pour some coffee into you.'

I felt myself grip tight to the seatbelt. 'There's a Little Chef on the A77.' He smiled. I didn't see what was funny. 'What have I said?'

'That shut years ago ... how long have you been away?'

I didn't want to answer that. The thoughts of Ulster and Claire were still rattling around in my head. 'Maybe too long.'

'You don't mean that? You couldn't wait to get away ...'

'That was then.'

Mason edged into the middle of the road and applied the brakes. We were at a roundabout. 'Are you seriously telling me you're glad to be back?'

I turned, watched him spin the wheel through his hands and edge towards the exit. 'Well, apart from this ...' I lifted my plaster cast, clattered it off the dashboard.

Mason had no reply. Even in my addled and inebriated state I could tell he harboured some shame about my injury. I allowed myself a vestige of gratitude for that: it could work in my favour. I needed Mason. I needed someone inside the force who could get to the bottom of who was looking after Jonny Gilmour and Councillor Crawford. I knew it went beyond a rogue officer or two – this was an organised affair. Too much was going on for it not to be; too much money was involved. If Ulster had taught me one thing, it was that money brought some serious players to the table.

We pulled up outside the Little Chef and Mason dragged himself from the car. He walked round to my side of the motor and pulled open the door. 'Can you walk?'

'Are you kidding?' As I rose from my seat, I began to doubt my cockiness. My legs felt light, my knees buckling beneath me. Mason put a hand on my elbow; I jerked it away. We somehow managed to make it through the car park and into an empty booth in the corner of the restaurant. Mason went for the coffees and returned with a large cup in each hand. He sat them both in front of me.

'Drink up,' he said.

I ventured a sip, then a couple more. The pressure behind my eyes began to ease. Mason seemed to be pleased but looked like he had something on his mind.

'What's up?' I said.

'What do you mean?'

'I've known you long enough to know when you've got a bug up your backside ... you used to wear that face when we were on the night beat together.'

He smiled. 'Can't kid a kidder, eh.'

'That's what they say.' I took another sip of coffee and waited for him to get down to brass-tacks.

'Remember I told you I did some checking on you?'

I did. He'd asked questions about my release from the RUC; I still wasn't happy about that. 'You could have just asked me, mate.'

He leaned forward, placed his elbows on the table. He dropped his voice as he spoke. 'Well, I'm asking now.'

I didn't know where to begin. Rabbie's words: *dare to be honest and fear no labour* seemed a good place to start. But, what had happened in Ulster? I was still searching for the answer to that one myself. All I did know was that I'd messed up. I'd refused to toe the line and it cost me everything I'd ever worked for. 'You know I was ... embedded.'

'Yeah, I got that much ... a loyalist mob.'

I huffed; there was no loyalty amongst criminals. 'They were a rabble. Just a gang with a lot of unsavoury activities going on ... the idea was for me to get to know them, get accepted.'

'And did you?'

I shook my head at the memory. 'Like a brother ...'

I could tell I had Mason rapt; his attention was almost laser-guided. 'So, tell me how it went wrong.'

'I made a discovery that didn't sit well with me, a discovery about the top man ...'

'The ganglord?'

'So to speak ...'

'What do you mean?'

I felt my jaw tightening at the recollection of the night I'd discovered Riley's core business wasn't the drug dealing we thought – or the gun running, or the prostitution. 'He supplied girls.'

'He was a pimp, you mean?'

I looked away, stared into the grey pool of coffee that sat in the bottom of the cup. 'No, I mean he supplied girls.' I looked up from my cup, stared into Mason's eyes. 'Young girls. Eight. Nine. Ten years old.'

'Jesus ...'

I saw Riley's face again, clear as rain in my mind. He was a monster, a beast. 'I told my boss, but he didn't want to do anything. So I told his boss and I was given the order to back off.' I tapped my spoon off the edge of the cup; the noise seemed to settle me. 'I was told, *ordered*, to sit tight and think of the bigger picture.'

Mason ran his large hand through his hair. 'I take it you didn't.'

'How the hell could I?' I threw down the spoon.

'Well, I know how this story ends ... so what did you do?'

'If you know how it ends, you'll know Riley was shot.'

'By you?'

'No! God, no.'

'But you know who did it?'

I stood up. The legs of the chair scraped noisily along the floor as I pushed away from the table. 'Mason, you've no right to ask me that ...'

He rose, fronted up to me. 'Why? Because the answer makes you a criminal too?'

I felt the muscles of my neck tighten as I gripped my jaw tight. 'Because there are some things in our line of work that you can never reveal. No matter what. You know that.'

He backed off. 'An eye for an eye, is that it, Doug?'

I forced a sarcastic laugh. 'You're kidding. Even I know that an eye for an eye leaves half the world blind.'

Chapter 22

Something my time in the RUC taught me was how to sober up in a hurry; your life could depend on it. I didn't know what was holding me back now. The dark thoughts? The sight of Mason looming over me? Or the fear of sobering up and realising my situation was every bit as bad as I feared? But I wanted to remain out of it.

I tapped my plaster cast off the table and swept aside the near-empty cup of coffee. 'I'm through.'

'I see that.' Mason raised an eyebrow as he spoke.

'I mean with the coffee.'

'Just get it down you, Doug.'

I looked up; he was frowning now. It was an expression I remembered from my school days back at Ayr Academy when teachers tired of asking nicely. The next step was going up a notch on the consequence scale. I raised the cup and downed the last of the grey liquid; the taste of cold coffee made me wince.

'Happy now?' I said.

Mason bit. 'I wouldn't go that far.' He rose from the table, started to fasten his jacket. 'Right, let's get you home.'

'Don't you want to … discuss things some more?'

Headshakes. 'Not tonight. You're in no fit shape. Besides, I think we've done enough talking.'

I stood to face him, made sure I was at my full height – somewhat shy of Mason's. 'You mean the time's come for action?'

'Maybe it has, but if that's the case, the next move's mine.'

I felt my gaze shifting, my eyes narrowing to discern the hint of a change in expression. I knew what he meant, but I had no idea what he was planning. Somehow, the thought of Mason taking matters into his own hands buoyed my excitement level. I was a child at heart. I envisaged him running amok in the station, smacking heads, like an elephant in a state of musth.

'And what about this Councillor Crawford?' I said.

'What about him?'

'Who's going to take care of him?'

Mason turned for the door, but managed a few words in my direction. 'The Craft take care of their own.'

I knew what he was saying: Crawford had brought far too much heat down on himself. Drugs busts were one thing; murder was a whole other level. The Craft didn't survive this long without some hint of self-preservation. They'd hang Crawford out to dry before they let anyone bring opprobrium to their doorstep.

We headed out to the car park. A soft rain fell, gathering in shallow pools on the tarmac. Passing vehicles created a momentary floodlight effect on our path to the car, showing up a silver motor that looked familiar.

'Hang about,' I said.

Mason stopped in his tracks. 'What is it?'

I remove a Marlboro and lit up. 'That's a Lexus over there.'

Mason shrugged. 'So?'

'You know who drives one of them?'

Another shrug.

'Gilmour.'

The mention of Jonny Gilmour changed the expression on his face. Mason strode out into the car park in the direction of the car. I put away my cigarette, jogged to catch him. As we started to run, the car's engine bit, the headlamps went on.

'He's clocked us,' I said.

Mason didn't reply, lunged for the door handle and pulled it open. 'Hello, Jonny …'

Gilmour sneered from behind the steering wheel, tipped his head forward and looked over the car park towards the traffic. 'What are you doing?' he said.

I squeezed past Mason, grabbed Gilmour by the collar. 'When did you get bold enough to ask the questions, mate?'

He eyeballed me. 'I'm not your mate. And you're not police, so get your hands off me.'

I felt a hand on my shoulder, gentle at first, then firmer. I was pulled out of the way by Mason. 'No he's not,' he said. 'But I sure as hell am!'

Mason reached into the Lexus and grabbed hold of Gilmour. There was a momentary flailing of arms as he was jerked from the driver's seat and deposited on the tarmac. He put out his hands, but his arms buckled at the elbows. He fell face first onto the ground, landing on his nose and chin. For a second or two he perched on his knees, in mock genuflection, then he raised his head and exposed the bloodied nose.

He put a hand to his face as he spoke. 'You're going to pay for this.'

I answered him. 'I doubt that, *mate*.'

'You've no idea who you're dealing with … no idea.'

I felt an urge to laugh, stifled it. I smiled. 'Have you?' I closed the two steps before us, grabbed Gilmour by the collar again. 'Do you think we don't know what's gone on here? Do you think you're dealing with Haud-it 'n' Dod-it?

We have your number, Gilmour ... we know you of old and don't think because you've made a few new friends that they're going to look after you. Because you'd be mistaken.'

He swiped at my hand, jumped to his feet. I could sense the red mist descending. He was ready to blow, but something held him back as he wiped blood from beneath his nose with the back of his hand.

I heard Mason move behind me. 'He's right, Gilmour. New friendships are fragile things. Slightest little misdemeanour and they're over.'

Gilmour kept his stare on me. 'What's he on about?'

There was little more than a gap of inches between us. I closed it further as I spoke through gritted teeth. 'He's on about the murder of Kirsty Donald.'

The whites of his eyes flashed as his focus shifted from my face to Mason's. 'You can't pin that on me.'

I reached out my hand, grabbed Gilmour's face in it. 'You've no idea what we can and can't do.'

He knocked me away, wiped the blood from beneath his nose again and stepped back. He started to point, first at me then at Mason. 'I'll have the pair of you.' He stepped back, made the shape of a gun with his fingers and levelled it towards us as he headed towards his car. 'I'll have the pair of you.'

Mason and I watched him slam the door of his car; he engaged the clutch and took first gear, wheels spinning. We followed the red tail-lights until they left the car park and faded out of sight.

'Do you think he's serious?' said Mason.

I turned to face him; the noiseless rain had covered his shoulders in damp little pinpricks. 'I hope so.'

'What?' He reached over and grabbed my plaster cast. 'Have you forgotten how you got this?'

I let the stookie fall from his hand. 'Ah, but this time ... we'll be waiting.'

Chapter 23

I'd once read something about Man being a genius strapped to a dying animal. I didn't feel much like a genius this morning but the dying animal part was painfully accurate. I rolled on my side and exhaled a slow, stilted breath. Somewhere inside my chest there was a heart beating. But it was struggling. My lungs didn't want to obey either: merely reaching for air took energy levels I didn't possess. My back and sides ached like I'd been worked over with a cricket bat, furiously; and my legs felt as immoveable as two ton-weights.

I somehow mustered a residue of strength to rub a cold palm over the side of my face and the gesture was enough to rob me of what little force I'd conserved from my night on the sauce. A thought came flooding in: I was too old for this caper. Far too old. At close to forty, it was time to surrender the foibles of youth. There had been a time when the first drink was like welcoming an old friend. He dropped by – usually at night – and the troubles of the day were soon forgotten. But those times were gone, past. The relief my old pal had once brought me had been supplanted with a nagging harpie who sat at my shoulder for days afterwards, telling me how stupid I was.

The curtains started to blow into the cold room. What

had once been little more than a draft was now replaced by a pernicious gale that brought a rattle to the window panes and tested the latch. I shivered as I watched the curtains rise, then subside. I could hear the suck and wash of the sea outside on the shore front and wondered how far I was from the elements. It felt as though only a thin layer of brick, on top of a thinner layer of plaster, separated us. The cold penetrated the duvet and blankets and set up lodgings in my bones. I couldn't bear it any longer; I knew it would take all my strength, all my resolve, to move from the bed. But I had to. There was another reminder of my stupidity forcing its way from the back of my mind to the front: the car park confrontation with Jonny Gilmour.

Mrs Kerr kept a fire burning downstairs; it was a ruse, of course, designed to tempt potential guests into staying. As I descended the final step of the broad staircase I saw her tending bar at the other end of the room. She still wore the tabard she had on day and night, and her hair was scraped back from her brow in the usual fashion; but there was something different about her. It was hard to spot, almost imperceptible to the unaccustomed, but to a drinker it was as good as a neon sign. Mrs Kerr wore her old-world disdain with a pride that her generation had failed to pass on to mine. She was a sherry-at-Christmas sort; maybe a small glass of bubbly to wet a baby's head. The idea of imbibing enough of the hard stuff to knock you out was anathema to her. She would never say it to me; but then, with those eyes burning it into me, she would never need to.

'Hello, Mrs Kerr,' I said.

She turned towards the clock on the wall. 'You've missed breakfast.'

I knew I had missed breakfast – and she knew that I knew – but that wasn't why she mentioned it. The time of my first appearance of the day was the issue she was subtly trying to draw attention to. 'I'm not very hungry.'

She picked up a glass from the bar, started to polish it with a white teatowel. 'No, I suppose you wouldn't be.'

I felt a fire ignite in my belly and a burning trail passed through my chest and onto my neck. She seemed to be going for broke. I wondered if I had really been all that bad. I'd got drunk alone, in my room, and then Mason whisked me away to the Little Chef. I tried to piece together the jigsaw of my memories but the moments between him knocking at my door and my arrival at the restaurant were missing. I knew, potentially, this meant I could have provided Mrs Kerr with quite enough ammunition to fire in my direction.

'I suppose you'd like a coffee.' She put a stinging inflection in her last word.

I avoided her eyes. 'Yes, that would be lovely. Thank you.'

As she turned towards the coffee-pot I removed my gaze from the floor and took in the scene of Queens Terrace. It was a broad street and the bay window provided a view of the whole sweep, all the way to the County Buildings. I thought about taking a walk. I might get as far as the Golden Disk, or if I was lucky enough, I could follow the Low Green down to the Fairfield House and grab a heart-starter. I was still daydreaming about getting myself back on track when a coffee cup was clattered before me and Mrs Kerr spoke once more.

'You had a visitor here last night.'

I reached for the coffee; the cup was hot. 'Yes, Mason. We used to be on the force together.'

She gave an audible sigh. 'No, I don't mean him.'

The first hit of caffeine made my head throb. 'You mean another visitor … after I left?'

The white tea towel was picked up again; the same glass

was picked up also. 'A woman.'

I lowered my coffee cup. 'That would have been Lyn.'

'That's not the name I was given.'

I was confused; the gnawing ache in my temples migrated to the base of my skull. The only other woman who knew I was here was my mother – I'd written the details down beside her telephone in case of emergencies; I doubted she would make a night visit to see me though. 'What name?'

Mrs Kerr stopped polishing the glass. 'Her name was Claire … she said she was your sister.'

'What? Claire … all the way from Inverness?'

'That's right. She waited for a bit but then she left.'

I was confused. I raised a hand to my head and scratched at my scalp. 'Well, did she leave a message?'

The audible sigh returned. Mrs Kerr's head tilted towards her shoulder in a gesture that could only be topped by snook cocking. 'She was a little irate after waiting for you to return, Mr Michie … in the end she said she would leave you a telephone message.'

I put my hand into my pocket and removed my mobile phone: the battery had died. The charger was upstairs in my room. I looked at my coffee cup on the bar, then back at Mrs Kerr. 'I'll have to check this.' I held up the phone. 'I'll come back for the coffee.'

She curled down her lips and looked away as I headed off. Why would my sister suddenly show up in Ayr? We'd exchanged some harsh words recently but I didn't expect her to show up and bawl me out for my insensitivity.

My hand was trembling a little as I reached out for my bedroom doorhandle. The hinges shrieked as I entered. The phone charger was where I'd left it, on the dresser, plugged into the wall. I connected my phone and waited for the green light to show that it was charging. In a moment the rest of the screen lit and my messages started to drop in. I scanned them briefly and clicked on the one with my sister's name beside the 'five missed calls' banner.

I dialled my voicemail.

'Doug … it's Claire, where are you?'

The line clicked off.

The next message queued up: 'Doug, Claire again, can you get back as soon as possible please? I need to talk to you.'

She sounded flustered, stressed.

The next call was empty. I heard her slam down a hard handset – a land-line.

The fourth call was the last one I listened to: 'Doug, I don't know where you are … Look, I came to your hotel … You need to get yourself to the hospital. It's mum. I'm afraid it's not good. Not good at all …'

Chapter 24

I hated hospitals more than any other place on Earth. I could still remember when they started building the new Ayr Hospital out at the Dalmellington Road. It seemed such a huge task, it would never be finished. There had been those that bemoaned the loss of smaller, friendlier establishments but the debate had been wasted on me. Hospitals were a place to be avoided at all costs. I loathed the harshly over-lit corridors, the smell of industrial antiseptic and bleach. More than that, I despised the proximity to death. Just pulling up in the car park made me feel coldly mortal.

As I headed for the front steps an old man shuffled through the door. He was wearing a heavy, checked dressing gown; one arm was attached to a bizarre looking pole on what looked like shopping-trolley wheels. At the top of the pole was a small, box-shaped bag containing some kind of clear liquid that made its way into his arm through a length of tubing. He seemed perfectly at ease with the apparatus, as if he'd been lugging it around his whole life.

'Excuse me, son.'

He'd caught me off guard. I turned my gaze from him, then quickly back. 'Yes …'

He fumbled with something in the pocket of his dressing

gown. When he gave up, I spotted his gnarled, arthritic fingers. 'You couldn't get a hold of the fags in there, could you?'

I smiled. 'Sure.'

A packet of B&H, the long ones – 100s. I opened them up, removed one and offered it to him.

'Could you light it for me, son?'

I clamped the cig in my mouth and sparked it up. The taste drew my attention, had me gasping for one myself. I resisted: had a feeling this bloke was capable of talking the leg off an iron pot, and I had my mother to attend to.

I passed over the cigarette, watched him suck in his sallow cheeks and slowly roll his eyes back in time to the tilt of his neck. A weak, thin hand like a claw was raised in a grim salute of thanks. I nodded and headed for the door.

My heart rate ticked into a speedy incline that verged on panic as I got inside. When I was on the force I had always hated visits to the hospital. Invariably, appearing at the infirmary meant something had gone wrong. There was only one place I dreaded more: the morgue, but visits there came with warning; you had time to prepare yourself for what was coming. And death carried an air of unreality. It seemed as distant as dreams to the living. Hospitals were firmly rooted in the now and appeared altogether more personal. You couldn't escape the incriminations of the patient you had come to see when they were lying before you. Even the beeps and whirs of medical machines spoke volumes in such situations.

I had come to see my own flesh and blood this time. As I approached the reception desk I felt my fists bunching in my coat pockets. Not from anger, but sheer anxiety. I knew my mother was in a bad way, had needed help, but I felt the most enormous guilt that I hadn't done more.

'Yes, can I help you?' The woman behind the counter had a kind face; she didn't look like a nurse. I'd always found them to be tough customers.

'Erm …' My mind went blank. I removed a hand, scratched the side of my head. My eyes scanned the woman in front of me again. She was smiling now. I dropped my gaze again. It fell on a name tag: Agnes McNeil.

'Are you visiting?' she said.

I took a breath, seemed to find focus. 'Yes, my mother … Michie, the name's Mich–'

She rose from her seat and placed a cold hand over my own. 'I think I know the lady.'

Agnes walked me to the lift. There were directions uttered but I let them whiz past like cyclists in a velodrome. I stored the room number and relied on instinct to lead me there. Once outside the door I tried to gather my thoughts but they were eclipsed by a surge of adrenalin. My breathing faltered again; my heartrate ramped.

Suddenly the door eased open.

'You're here …' It was Claire.

'Yes …' A ridiculous reply to a ridiculous question.

Claire pressed her thin frame through the door and placed a hand on my chest; she was motioning me away from the room.

'I think we should make our way down the corridor …' Claire's eyes flitted, first to the left and then the right. The gesture made me dizzy.

'What?' I was confused. I'd come to see my mother.

'There's a room … one of those waiting rooms, I've just lost my bearings.' She took my arm, started to walk me down the cold, bright corridor. I heard her heels clack on the hard flooring. Her hair swished on her shoulders as she turned her head from left to right scanning the glass-fronted doors on the ward. 'I've seen it, I know it's here.'

I wanted to grab my sister by the shoulders, spin her round and return to the room my mother was in. 'Claire, I came here to see Mam.'

She reached out, grabbed a handle and flung open the door it was attached to. 'Let's get a coffee.'

'Did you hear me?'

'Doug, please.' Her voice rose. 'Can we just go inside … ?' She pointed into the open room; grey-blue carpet tiles on the floor looked primed with static. A tall vending machine with Twix and Mars and McCoy's crisps sat against the wall.

'I only want to see our mother, Claire. Why have you dragged me away?'

Her thin lips started to tremble. She looked down towards the floor. 'You can't.'

My chest inflated. 'What do you mean, *I can't?*'

She folded her arms, gripped herself. She looked so small, a waif, like a schoolgirl. She tilted her head to the side and rubbed at the edges of her arms. The slow tremble of her lips seemed to disappear as she tried to speak again. But nothing came.

I didn't need to hear the words.

I turned away and set off through the corridor towards my mother's room. My steps were dull, flat thuds on the flooring, my legs almost too stiff to move as I struggled back the way we'd come just a few moments before, only now I carried a heavy weight of new knowledge in my mind.

Claire cried out. 'Doug … no, please.'

I waved her away. She ran behind me and grasped onto my coatsleeve. 'Doug, Doug …'

At the door she'd squeezed through earlier, Claire backed off. I turned to see her shivering against the wall. She looked away. I stepped inside and caught sight of my mother in the bed. Her head was pointed towards the ceiling, her mouth agape. Her skin, as thin as paper, was pale and yellowed. She was still. She looked like a stranger to me, She was certainly no longer my mother; her spirit had gone.

Chapter 25

The drive back to my guest house in Queens Terrace passed in a blur. The greatest surprise to me was that I genuinely found it difficult to mourn for my mother. The woman who had raised me, who had cared for me and taught me as a child, had died a long time ago. I hardly recognised the person she had become. Drinking herself to a stupor, spouting bitter recriminations in every direction for the collapse of her once happy life was bad enough to see, but the lack of self-respect left us all bewildered.

I had tried to look at her as she lay on the hospital bed, tried to discern some hint of her emotion, but I couldn't register a glimmer of recognition. I couldn't help but believe the drinking, the dissipation, was the final chapter she had chosen for herself. It was a long slow suicide and we all took part. Me, my sister, the health authorities, social services. We were powerless to halt her fall. The decision was all hers.

In the force, I had watched people dive to the bottom of a whisky bottle every night of the week. Early on I'd seen the futility of intervention: how do you protect a man from himself? Their fate was theirs to control alone. Rabbie had put it more eloquently and his words gathered steam in my mind now: *nae man can tether time nor tide*. None indeed.

I parked up and went inside the guest house. Mrs Kerr spotted me from beyond the bar; she raised a delicate hand and then, slowly, smiled. The smile seemed to be tempered with sympathy; she touched the edge of her mouth and kept me in her gaze for a moment longer and then I broke for the stairs. I knew she had averred a change in me since we last spoke: my grief – or was it guilt? – was written all over me.

I removed my bag from the wardrobe and packed my few things quickly. I left the bedroom door slightly ajar, the keys sitting on the sidetable. I would settle my account in full later; Mrs Kerr knew I was good for it, and that I was in no shape for conversation right now.

On the way out to Alloway the traffic slowed along the Maybole Road as workers dug up a new stretch. It would be gas mains, or new cables of some description going in. The road's tarred surface was a battle-scarred mess of riven mounds and deep cleaves. An old man with a Westie dog stood shaking his head by the temporary traffic lights. His hair was as white as the dog's, probably too white for his age, but I envied him his years on behalf of my mother.

As the lights changed I planted the foot and turned onto Laughlanglen Road. The long dipping sweep of the thoroughfare took in a children's play area with slides and swings on one side and the grassy hills of Rozelle Park on the other. I remembered as a child watching a man in a Porsche pull up and commence batting golf balls into the park as the children ran to collect them up. It seemed like a million years ago. Pre-time. But it happened. I knew it happened because I held the memory in my mind. I wondered what thoughts and memories that my mother had once held had now died with her?

At the family home my sister's car was in the driveway. It was only a small Fiesta but she had managed to take up the entire two-car capacity. I flicked on the blinkers and parked with two wheels hanging over the kerb. Claire appeared at the door with her bags as I emerged from the Audi.

'Hello, Doug.'

I nodded. 'Nippy, isn't it?'

Claire's eyes widened momentarily and then she put down her bags. 'Will I make you a coffee?'

I stepped forward. We were trapped in our own unease. 'No, you get away. Get back to your kids ... it's a fair drive you have.'

She shook her head. 'I can hang on a wee bit. For a coffee.' She seemed to doubt her words; her lashes batted quickly. 'I mean, I'll be back to help with the ... arrangements. Obviously.'

'Claire, it's fine ... honestly.'

She sighed, loudly. I reached out a hand and rubbed at her shoulder. 'Maybe a wee coffee before you get up the road then, eh?'

She nodded and we went inside.

The house had that familiar musty smell that I'd grown used to of late. It was a combination of the lack of dusting and airing teamed with general neglect. As I looked around I waited for Ben to appear, to come lolling from side to side, bumping his way along the walls in his blindness.

'Where's the dog?' I said.

'Out the back.' Claire began to fill the kettle. 'I did wonder what to do with him.'

'He's fine with me.'

'Are you sure? It's a lot of responsibility and he's getting on.' She looked like she wished she could snatch back her words.

'He's fine with me. Look, one of us needs to get the house in order and ...'

'I will help you, Doug.'

I removed one of the stools from beneath the breakfast bar and sat down. 'You can leave the funeral arrangements to me.'

She clunked two cups on the work surface. 'I think she had a policy … y'know, insurance. Dad had one of them.'

I nodded. 'I'll look it out. Don't worry about it.'

The kettle started to whistle. Claire leaned against the sink. I noticed her fingernails gripping the stainless-steel edge. 'Doug, you don't think she held anything against us, do you?'

How did I answer that? I knew she held everything against everyone. It's what she had become. The world didn't suit her anymore. 'No, Claire, I'm sure she didn't.'

My sister started to pick at the sink's edge. 'She had so much anger, I couldn't handle it. The lashing out, it really hurt me. She missed the kids' birthdays year after year and I resented her. I felt bad for that, but …'

I got off the stool, walked towards my sister and took her in my arms. 'Claire, we all felt resentment. It's hard. We lost her a long time ago.'

She started to whimper; she dipped her head and sobbed onto my chest. I held onto her but I didn't know what to say or do. 'But we've lost her twice, Doug … we lost her then, when she changed, and we've lost her again now.'

I longed for the right thing to say, to make things right for Claire but there was no way of patching over this. Everything she said was true. 'I know, I know.' It was all I could say.

Chapter 26

It was a beautiful Ayrshire morning: blue skies and birdsong. I stuck my head out the front door to see if I was mistaken, but no, there was no hint of rain in the air. All was quiet. All was still. At least, outside. I was being eaten up inside about my reaction to the death of my mother. I wanted to feel more, but I couldn't help but see her death as a blessing. The way she had been living was no life at all.

I made coffee, replaced the crispness of the morning air with the harsher tang of Nescafé instant. I toyed with the idea of breakfast, some eggs maybe. Toast perhaps. The stookie on my arm would make anything more complicated a trial. In the end I decided that my stomach wasn't up to it and stayed with the coffee. Ben was anxious to get out, to stretch his old legs and relieve his no-doubt aching bladder. I ruffled his ears in consolation for a moment but then the whimpering started.

'Okay, boy … you win.'

My coat still carried a hint of the heady antiseptic smell it had picked up in the hospital the day before. I winced a little on first contact but flung it on. The old dog managed to claw at his lead as I attached it to his collar. We set out for the slim strip of woods that skirted the edge of Pemberton Valley.

The ground carried a slight dusting of frost that covered footprints and puddles with a layer of glassy ice. I crunched a few underfoot as the dog shuffled along, sniffing and rasping as the lead strained. It was good to be out; walking always cleared the mind. At least, let you think that for a short time. I knew my darker thoughts were waiting to attack me back at my mother's house.

As the trees started to thin out and The Loaning came into view, I felt myself returning to civilization; the serried ranks of bungalows and detached villas appeared all too soon. At the bus shelter I toyed with the idea of going deeper into the woods but I could see by the heavy breath bursting from Ben that he'd had enough. We returned to our slow pace on the pavement, the sound of the dog's claws scraping on the frosty flags.

We'd managed only a short distance when I started to hear a car crawling behind us. I turned, caught sight of a white Nissan Almera. It had been pimped up, the suspension lowered and a ridiculous spoiler stuck on the back. Behind the wheel was a young lad in his early twenties. He had a short, all-over crop and broad shoulders. He was glowering at me, thinned eyes beneath Neanderthal 'brows. The sight of him set my pulse quickening. The sight of his friend in the seat beside him, unravelling what looked like a machete from a Tesco carrier was the real shock though.

I halted in my tracks. Stood still on the road and put the bead on them. There was some grit about the pair, but I knew the type. They were on wages. Any trouble they had with me wasn't their own. I could use that to my advantage.

I tied the dog to a gatepost at the foot of one of the facsimile driveways and returned to my stance on the pavement, directing my glare into the car's windscreen. The pair kept eyes on me but didn't flinch. As I sized them up, guessed their age and what possible experience they might have, I found them lacking. I chanced my luck.

As I walked towards the Almera I stared to remove my

wristwatch. I made a show of depositing the item in my pocket and then I undid the top button of my coat and inserted my hand. All the while I kept my eyes on the pair of mugs. They thought I was carrying; holding a weapon that was at least the match of theirs. It was a move I knew you could only get away with when the targets were wet behind the ears.

I was chancing my luck.

But it worked.

The driver spun wheels and took off up The Loaning, racing through the gears. I watched them go and caught sight of the one nearest me drawing the machete across his throat in a blatant threat. I smiled, pretended to be unfazed, like this sort of thing was meat and drink to me.

I watched the car disappear into the distance, reach the point where the road met the school and turn sharply towards the by-pass. I was perplexed, but I knew I shouldn't be surprised by this sudden escalation of events. Gilmour had warned me. The cops in balaclavas had warned me. And Crawford had warned me. Something about chickens coming home to roost rung true.

I turned for home, unhooked the dog's lead and adopted a slow stroll that belied my churning insides. By the time we reached the door to my mother's home, I'd been through a list of possibilities. I watched as Ben lapped at his water bowl and then I hunted down my mobile phone. I had to make a call urgently.

I brought up my contacts and located the number I was looking for.

Ringing.

'Come on, Lyn ... pick up!'

She answered on the fourth ring. 'Doug?'

'Yeah, how are you?'

She huffed. 'Just peachy. How do you think?'

Immediately I saw the stupidity of my opener. I needed to tread carefully. She was likely to be as agitated as me by recent events. And to add to her woes, she had a son in custody to think of.

'I have some news for you ...'

'You do?' her voice was high, hopeful.

'It's not good news ... My mother passed away.'

'Oh, Doug ...' She changed her tone, seemed stronger somehow. I had shaken her from self-absorption.

'It was very sudden.'

'I'm so sorry. If there's anything I can do.'

I moved the phone to my other hand. 'There is something.'

'Name it ...'

'Well, you might not like it, but I think it would be for the best in the circumstances.'

A gap opened on the line, stretched over a few seconds, then, 'I'm not with you.'

'I need you to leave town.'

'*What?*'

I knew this was the reaction I could expect. 'Do you have a friend or family that you can go and stay with for a few days?'

'Well, there's my sister on Arran ... but I don't understand.'

I felt my back muscles stiffen. I was tensing. I knew how serious matters had got and I was worried for Lyn's safety; but I couldn't panic her. I needed to shield her from the worst of what was to come. She had been through enough. 'I think, to be on the safe side, I'd just like you to be somewhere else. For a little while, anyway.'

'But it doesn't make sense, I've been with you from the start and you know how I feel about –'

'Lyn, you need to leave town. It won't be forever, but I need to ask you to do this ... now.'

Chapter 27

I wouldn't exactly call it fear but there was certainly a new level of caution infecting my every move. I'd seen some things in Ulster, seen how the border towns dealt with threats, how the police stations had to be kitted out with a portcullis, barricades and barrels of razor wire to keep grudges at bay. I wasn't about to go that far, but I wasn't waiting for the next mug with a machete to come knocking either.

In Ayr there had always been types who would do things you couldn't dream up in your worst nightmares for a few quid. I'd known hard men who fancied their chances taken down by chib-carrying gangs of yobs – the rent-a-mob, bribed with Staffie pups or bags of grass. A tin of Cally Special could pay for a glassing in some pubs. It was the low end of the market and ultimately the most unpredictable. I had too much going on, was too close to the truth of Kirsty Donald's murder, to be on guard round the clock, but I knew what to do about it.

I took a drive out to Tam's Brig, parked up and walked back the way I'd come, past Virginia Gardens. I liked the Tam's Brig area. It had a schizophrenic feel; being wedged between Ayr and Prestwick it never quite knew whether to be on the way up, or the way down. I knew what I wanted it to be though, as I set out towards the shady bedsits that studded the fag-end of the Auld Toun.

I took a wee lane, a wynd off the corner where the old chippie used to sit. I could see the Davis Snooker Club from where I was standing and it drew to mind the night I'd spotted Gilmour and Crawford leaving there. I shook my head, muttered, 'Upped the ante, eh lads?'

They certainly had, but they didn't know who or what they were dealing with. I'd brought down bigger, and bolder. Far bolder. True, I had better back up then, but I shoved that to the farthest reaches of my mind. There was no place for doubts where I was going.

As I knocked on the door some flakes of dry white paint fluttered to the ground. I heard movement, chair legs dragging, and then a tobacco-stained net-curtain was yanked back from the window. I watched Broonie clock me, take in that I was not a threat and then move towards the door.

He opened up, but kept the chain on. He checked out the stookie on my arm. 'What the hell do you want?'

I kept my voice low, but definite. 'A shooter.'

'Jesus!' He slammed the door. The chain rattled and then the wood was jerked back again. Broonie grabbed me, pulled me inside. 'What are you playing at?'

I looked him up and down. He was wearing an ancient Frankie Says T-shirt and chewing-gum coloured Y-fronts; the backside was falling out of them. 'Come on, don't mess me about. Are you holding or not? If you're not, I want to know who is.' I reached inside my jacket, removed a bundle of notes I'd tied tightly with an elastic band. 'I'm paying cash for a quick sale. Today, Broonie.'

The bedsit was tiny, beyond cramped. I checked out the pile of dishes sitting in the far corner. A boxy television, so old it had a wood-veneer, fizzed beside it. The place stank of puff and fortified wine that clung to the air making for a sticky, heady miasma.

Broonie picked at his elbow and shivered. 'What you on about, man ... I don't hold shooters.'

I looked down at his bare feet. I was tempted to stamp on his toes, hard, just to remind him who he was talking to. That kind of thing once came as second nature to me but the older I got I found using my mind, and words, was a little more effective.

'I'm not polis anymore ... you know that?'

'Aye, I heard ... heard quite a bit about you lately.' Broonie backed up, started to move upended Buckfast bottles from the coffee table as he hunted for a fag. I watched his search prove fruitless then I removed my pack, sparked him up. He took the cig and tucked his free hand under his armpit. 'Okay, now just suppose I did know somebody with a shooter, and I'm only saying, suppose ... what's in it for me?'

I had his number; started to peel off a crisp twenty from the roll, said, 'Well, I'd obviously be grateful.'

Broonie watched my hands, the sound of the notes – crisp and new – attracted his full attention. He lunged forward and took the bait.

'Wait here.' He pointed at me with the cig, moved towards a manky curtain that separated his living quarters from his sleeping area. I heard him rummaging about, then speaking into a phone briefly before returning in a jollier mood. In his hand was a small ASDA carrier, weighted down with something.

'Right, let's see the colour of yer money, Michie.'

I shook my head. 'I don't think that's the way it works, mate.'

A twitch in his eyebrow started to spread to the rest of his forehead. 'Right. Right ... 'sake, man.' He delved into the carrier, removed a small newspaper-covered package and handed it to me. I took the package – a fair weight –

and unwrapped the newspaper. Inside was a dirty oil-cloth; beneath that, a gun that looked like a museum piece.

'What's this?' I said.

'Five hundred.'

I laughed. 'If I take it on the Antiques Roadshow maybe.'

Broonie pinched his nose. 'That's Army-issue ... a Webley.'

I shook my head. I opened the chamber; it was empty.

Broonie spoke, 'Do you slugs for a pound a throw.'

I handed it back. 'I'll give you a ton and you can chuck in the ammo.'

'Two-fifty.'

'A ton-fifty.'

'Done.'

Felt like I had been.

I tucked the loaded weapon in my waistband and headed back to the car. I was in dangerous proximity to the John Street nick. Carrying a concealed weapon was a serious offence but I figured that if the local constabulary caught me with a shooter, I wouldn't be going to trial. It would be me or them.

In the car I removed the Webley and placed it inside the glove box. I turned over the ignition and found first gear. The car purred to life as I accelerated and headed back to the shore front. I had my next move mapped out. It involved a visit to the Port of Ayr, to another meet with Councillor Crawford. I knew he would put up fierce opposition to what I had to say, but I'd come prepared for that. This time I'd get the answers I wanted. Or else.

Chapter 28

Day was tipping into night. The dark waters lapping the port's edge reflected the street lamps; little iridescent pinpricks in a wriggling, slithering shoreline. I sat in the car and watched the colours – from heliotrope to hazy blackness – moving in hypnotic patches. I felt calmed, at ease. I was comfortable, but I knew I had no right to be. I was here for a reason and sitting in my car was merely prolonging the inevitable.

I closed my eyes, laid my head on the rim of the steering wheel. There were thoughts swirling about in my mind but not the ones I wanted. I wanted to find the words to bring Crawford down; to rattle him, have him calling for mercy. But I wasn't there yet. If this was a poker game I'd be holding jack; jack-high if I was lucky.

I tried to line up what I'd learned: the Port had seen some dodgy goings on; Crawford was being protected by the Craft; he had a connection to Gilmour; and there was my gut instinct that the lot of them where in cahoots for profit.

I'd seen the press reports with the endless busts at the port. The longstanding problem with smuggling there was so prevalent it was next-door to impossible to get my own brand of smokes in the Auld Toun. But what did I have on them? Nothing but suspicions. They knew I was onto them, but somehow, I wondered if I really worried them. There were the threats, the beating and the broken hand but that was small-time to them. A girl had been murdered: that's what they were really capable of.

I let out a sigh.

'Jesus, Doug, think, man ...' I was talking to myself. Who was rattled: them or me? I knew the answer and it scared the daylights out of me.

I was shook from my stupor by a knock on the car's window. I looked up and saw a young girl bent into the wind, long scarf trailing behind her like a pennant in the wind.

I rolled down the window. 'Jennifer ...'

She smiled. 'I was hoping to catch you again.'

Her conscience had returned then. 'You were?'

She looked back at the building she had just come from, then leaned in closer. 'Could we maybe go somewhere ... to talk?'

I nodded to the seat beside me. 'Jump in.'

As Jennifer slinked round the front of the Audi, I started the engine. She climbed in and fastened her seatbelt. 'How about the Horizon Hotel? It's about the nearest.'

She pinched her 'brows, turned down her eyelids. 'Could we maybe go a little further? I'd sooner not bump into anyone from, y'know, work.'

I got the message. 'Sure.'

I turned around, made for the top of the town. The traffic was heavy, lots of rush-hour commuters returning home to firesides and car-crash television. I glanced towards my passenger periodically. She was silent, but I caught her nibbling on her nails once or twice. She was on edge and I doubted that would play to my advantage. On the upside, she had chosen her moment. Seemed resolved to reveal something to me; I hoped she wouldn't bottle out.

'There's a place, a newish place I think, but I can't remember what it's called.' I tried to keep to small chat, to put her at ease. 'If I park up at Matalan, there's a wee lane we can take there. It's a nice place, lots of pictures on the walls, original art work.'

'I presume you're not talking about the wee lane …' She pasted on a thin smile. She didn't seem to be thawing any. 'It's called The Beresford.'

'That'll be it. It's on Beresford Terrace.'

When we reached our destination I picked a secluded spot at the far corner of the bar and ordered some coffee. Jennifer removed her scarf and opened her coat. She seemed uncomfortable, her legs crossed at an awkward angle, her shoulders tensed and board-stiff.

I waited for the coffees, then made my opening gambit. 'How have things been at the office?'

She huffed; her torso seemed to deflate. 'Since your last visit, you mean … How do you think?'

I tried not to think. I would do that afterwards. After she'd revealed what it was she wanted to tell me. 'Are you comfortable there, Jennifer? Would you not like to take off your coat? It's warm in here.'

She shook her head. 'I don't want to stay long.'

I nodded. 'That's fine. We can make this as brief as you like.'

She clanked down her coffee cup. Some grey liquid spilled over the edge of the saucer. 'Look, you know I spoke to Kirsty Donald. You know she came to the Port Authority with those complaints.'

I felt my eyes widen. 'Complaints?'

Jennifer was looking out the window. 'God, yes. Every other day, they got worse. Her dad was a builder, put up the flats. I think she was, y'know, worried about his investment … about what was going on.'

'And what was that, Jennifer?'

She seemed to clam up.

I reached out a hand, placed it on her arm. 'Kirsty paid a dear price for a few complaints to the Port Authority, don't you think?'

She drew deep breath. Her lips trembled over her words. 'I'm scared.'

I gripped her arm. 'It's the guilty who should be scared, Jennifer.'

Her eyes moistened as she started to speak again. 'Kirsty was on the site at all hours. She had a flat there, saw things. At first I jotted down all her concerns. Stuff like noise, y'know, the cranes they unload with and so on.'

'Go on …'

'No-one really seemed bothered but and then she complained about not being taken seriously. She'd jotted down times of late-night unloading, when they're not supposed to, and there were pictures.'

'You mean photographs?'

'Yes. It was like she was on a mission by then. That's when Councillor Crawford started to get … upset.'

'*Upset*?'

'I mean angry. There'd been the drugs seizures, the stuff that got in the papers about the illegal immigrants and he just lost it then. He didn't want any more bad press.'

'But Kirsty made official complaints, I take it?'

Jennifer stared deep into my eyes and then turned away. 'Well yes … and no.'

'I don't understand.'

Her voice was a low drawl; she seemed to be choking back tears, or the truth. Perhaps both. 'I got rid of the complaints.'

'What … how?'

She folded over, started to grip at her sides. 'Councillor

Crawford told me to remove them from the files.' Her voice jumped. 'I'm only admin, I have to do what I'm told!'

'Oh, no …' I slumped back in my seat.

Jennifer sat silently for a moment. She seemed to be weighing up something behind her teary gaze. 'I know I shouldn't have, it could cost me my job, but … I took them home anyway.'

I was lost. 'Took what home?'

'The copies. I was scared … so I made copies of all her complaints.'

Chapter 29

There was something about driving at night; it lured you into an altered sense of reality. I planted the foot, shot up the '77. The car felt like a capsule rocketing into space. The road ahead was an illusion of light-trails. Twisting, bending beams that stretched out like fireworks then suddenly sheared off with a tilt of the wheel. I followed the arc of lights through the Whitletts Roundabout and dropped down through the gears. The Auld Toun, fully lit, appeared anew to me, like this was the first time I'd really seen it. I was on a high, a natural high brought about by the pumping adrenalin surging through me.

On Heathfield Road I rolled down the window and the illusion was broken. Reality flooded in on the breeze. I became dimly aware of Bowie's *Lodger* on the CD player: the track was *Look Back in Anger*. I listened to the Thin White Duke. He was going on about waiting so long; I knew the territory.

I dropped the revs at the KFC and slowed into the second roundabout. The rest of the road, the glut of garages and semi-Ds served to bring me round to the idea that I was indeed back in Ayr. I hadn't imagined it, dreamt it up. I had come a long way from Ulster to this point and I wondered why I'd put myself through it. For what? For whom? I knew the answer I'd been trying to avoid: for Lyn.

On Prestwick Road I tried to re-wire my brain. I had taken the documents from Jennifer and I knew what to do with them. I scanned the side of the road for a post box; they were becoming increasingly scarce to find. I'd made copies of the complaints, shoved them into an A4 envelope and scribbled Mason's home address on it; if anything happened to me, the rest would be down to him.

Finally I spotted a post box, flicked on the blinkers, and pulled up.

I looked at the envelope in my hand, white against the stookie that was greying now, dirty. My handwriting was a messy scrawl. Nerves? I didn't doubt it. I applied the six or so first-class stamps I had bought and placed the envelope in the slot.

My heart was still pumping as I returned to the car.

I dialled Mason's number.

Ringing.

He answered in his usual manner. 'Yeah.'

'It's me.'

'Yeah … and?'

I squeezed the phone. 'There's been some … developments.'

He drew breath. 'Go on.'

I didn't know where to start, so skipped straight to the meat of the issue. 'Kirsty Donald made repeated complaints to the Port Authority, stuff about late-night unloading; strange characters coming and going; boat-loads of suspected illegals walking off the dock; contraband –'

'Hang about. How do you know this?'

I manoeuvred myself into the driving position, locked on my seatbelt. 'I have the official files. They were removed, supposedly deleted, but I got them.'

His voice rose. I heard the springs of his chair wheeze. 'How?'

'Never mind that for now.' I opened the glove box, took

out the Webley revolver. Placed it on the passenger seat. 'Mason, I'm taking care of this … tonight.'

His already loud voice reached a new pitch. 'Now hang on a minute, Doug!'

I picked up the shooter, tucked it inside my coat pocket. 'You'll have the documents – Kirsty Donald's complaints – in the next post. I doubt they'll secure a conviction on their own but they might, you know, set the cat amongst the pigeons.'

'And you're all about that malarkey, aren't you?'

I smiled into the phone. 'Thanks for everything, pal.'

'Doug, don't do anything stupid. Will you promise me that?'

'I don't do promises, Mason.'

I hung up.

I cranked the engine and set the wheels in motion. Bowie was on *Red Money* now. I turned the volume down. I didn't want to draw any attention to myself as I set out along Prestwick Road. I knew exactly where I needed to go. Jonny Gilmour had shown me the way in his silver Lexus the night he'd dropped Councillor Crawford off. I didn't imagine for a second I'd be a welcome house guest, but then I had the Webley to persuade him otherwise.

On the force, in Ulster, they had a saying: *you get further with a gun and kind words than just kind words.*

They had underestimated me, underestimated how far I would go to see the job done.

As I drove I thought of Lyn, of her son, Glenn. I thought of that day when I drove into Ayr and saw her standing in the rain at the Old Racecourse. She was wrecked, a broken woman. Life had taken something precious from her. It was a look I'd seen a thousand times before but it was the last thing I expected to see on my return home. I had wanted to escape all that: the hurts, the miseries. But fate didn't have that role in mind for me.

Christ, it wasn't out there for me. I banged on the brow of the steering wheel. They had my number from the off.

I knew in my heart that Lyn felt she'd found a kindred spirit – birds of a feather flock together and all that nonsense. But so had Mason. He'd tuned into my wavelength the second I told him about Riley and the girls, those eight, nine, ten-year-old girls. I saw Riley's face before me again; the beast made my stomach lurch.

I should have pulled that trigger.

I felt sickened by the world; by what I'd seen of it. I knew I'd let too much go, too much pass without the proper action being taken. I was tired of people being preyed upon, by the strong ruling the weak. Someone had set Glenn up to take a fall; it was all about preserving profits, about keeping their nice little earner going. They were worse than Rabbie's *parcel of rogues*.

Crawford's sandstone villa eased into view and I slowed the Audi, brought the car into the side of the road and dimmed the lights.

My hand was trembling as I killed the ignition.

I looked towards the villa; a light was burning downstairs.

I pressed the shooter to my ribs as I moved off.

Chapter 30

At the end of Councillor Crawford's drive was a pair of stone lions. They made me smile. At this point, a smile on my face was the last thing I was expecting. There had been a farcical case a few years ago where a similar set of stone lions had been swiped from the front of a hotel in the Auld Toun. The press had gone overboard on the theft but a few residents saw the funny side. The lions were given names and postcards from all over the world started coming into the papers signed Francie and Josie. One minute they were in Rio, the next Nantucket. I wondered now if the hotel ever got the lions back.

As I was smiling at the memory, I felt myself being watched. I tipped my head back and met Crawford's gaze. He was standing in the centre of his front room, speaking into a mobile phone. He recognised me immediately and walked to the window. I nodded towards him and made my way to the front door. He seemed, if not happy, at least content to see me on his property. His reaction baffled me because soon after our last meeting I had landed a broken hand.

I stood at the front door, listening to the chain being withdrawn, the key turning in the lock; it was a heavy mortise lock. As the door eased open I caught sight of

Crawford: he was wearing a cardigan and house slippers. He seemed relaxed; I didn't rate his chances of staying in that mood.

'Hello, Councillor.'

He positioned his glasses on his nose. 'Is this a business call?'

I suppressed a laugh. 'Well, let's just say, it isn't pleasure.'

He looked at me, seemed perplexed. A few stray hairs escaped from his smoothed-back fringe. 'I suppose I better invite you in, Mr Michie.'

'Oh, I suppose you better had, Councillor.'

We moved into a broad hallway. A sweeping balustrade curved upwards on one wall; a small table with an umbrella stand rested on the opposite wall. I walked over to the table and laid down the envelope containing the copies of Kirsty Donald's complaints to the Port Authority.

'That could be your bedtime reading. Only I wouldn't want to leave it that late to get stuck in, if I were you.'

Crawford's footsteps were silent as he crossed the black and white tiled floor towards the envelope. As he stretched out a hand, I noticed the heels of his socks were wearing thin. He removed his glasses and placed them in his shirt pocket; another, smaller set of half-moons was resting on strings round his neck. He perched them on his nose as he read.

'How did you come by this?' His tone was firm, cocky.

'What the hell does that matter? ... It won't change the outcome.'

He folded over the photocopies, re-inserted them in the envelope. He seemed to be slowing down, entering a different state of consciousness. I watched him choose his words carefully. 'Oh, I wasn't thinking it would. Not for a second.' He released a slow grimace. 'It was your outcome I was thinking about.'

I felt a fuse light behind my eyes. 'That's it!'

I removed the Webley and pointed it at Crawford. He lifted his hands, palms pointed at me. 'By God you're making a big mistake.'

'Oh, really?'

'Put the gun away. Please be sensible.'

I felt a line of sweat break on my brow. Another traced the length of my spine. 'You really are a piece of work, aren't you? Not content with knocking off Kirsty Donald for clocking your dodgy little operation, you think you can preach to me.'

He lowered his hands. 'You don't know what you're talking about.'

'Don't I? ... Then perhaps you should do some explaining ...' I took a step towards him, pointed the shooter at his ear. 'Fast!'

'Okay. Okay.' He backed off. 'Just put the gun down, please.'

I cocked the weapon. 'Be in no doubt, I'm not messing here, Councillor.'

His pallor dropped several shades; a grey tongue flashed over his dry lips. 'Th-the girl was nothing to do with me ... nothing!'

'I don't believe you.'

'It's the truth! I never wanted her hurt. Never.'

I felt my teeth grinding, spoke through my bottom row. 'Then who did? Gilmour? Was it him?'

Crawford backed onto the wall. I could see his heart beating hard beneath his shirt. 'It was her fault ... hers! She should have chosen her boyfriends more carefully.'

I raised the gun, smacked the butt of the handle into the wall. Some plaster chips fell to the floor in a shower of dust. 'Don't give me that. You and I both know Glenn had nothing to do with Kirsty's death.' I smacked the gun barrel off his cheek; a thin welt appeared, a trickle of dark blood beneath it.

Crawford raised his hands to his head and slid towards the floor. A broad line of sweat followed down the wall behind him. 'You don't know anything!'

I leaned over him, roared. 'Then enlighten me. Now! Because your time's running out.'

He looked up at me, his eyes bulging. 'You have the wrong man.'

I didn't want to hear any more. Sweat clogged my eyelids as I pressed the gun stalk to his head. 'Wrong answer!'

'No. Wait.' He showed palms again, trembled in pity for himself. 'I told him ...'

'Who?'

'Gilmour ... Jonny Gilmour. I told him not to go there. That she would know him, recognise him. Because of Glenn!'

I stepped back. '*What?*'

Crawford looked up. His intent eyes followed me as I retreated. 'You don't know, do you?' He raised himself on his haunches, then stood before me. 'Glenn is Gilmour's son.'

My thoughts swam. My head burned. I tried to steady myself on the banister, the gun heavy in my hand.

Crawford spoke, 'You didn't know. She never told you.' He started to grow in confidence. 'No. Of course she would keep something like that to herself.' He shook his head, laughed. 'She kept it from the boy for long enough, but he must've found out because the girl recognised Gilmour when he went round.'

Crawford kept mocking me as I shook my head and tried to block it all out.

'Lyn lied to you, Michie,' he laughed. 'She lied to you

because she knew you were a loser and would take it in.'

I turned away, my thoughts and emotions aflame.

'And you thought you'd found your dream woman,' Crawford laughed again. 'And all along it turns out she's just some cheap slut who led you on.'

I spun to face him. I knew at once he sensed the hurt in my eyes and the anger behind it; he seemed to enjoy the thrill even more. 'There'll be no future for you and that slut Lyn now ...' He was still laughing. 'I mean, who'd want a cheap slag who's had Jonny Gilmour between her legs ... a cheap lying slut who led you on and made a mad fool of you ...'

I raised the gun, levelled it towards him.

Crawford was oblivious of me, still grinning and gesticulating, still full of himself and his power. I didn't hear his words as I tightened my fist round the gun and pulled the trigger.

Chapter 31

I braced myself for the gun's loud report, the flashing muzzle and the resulting smoke – but nothing came. The hammer fell, made a resounding thud that was strong enough to shake the barrel, but no bullet appeared. I turned the weapon over, played with the mechanism; the time I took to do this was only a few seconds but they were vital seconds. As I looked up, Crawford had bolted for the front door. A breeze from the street sent a small pile of mail fluttering from the hallway table. I watched the brown and white envelopes – including Kirsty's complaints – float their way to the floor like Autumn leaves. I was still caught up in the unreality of the situation. I had aimed to shoot a man but somehow the rashness of the moment had been taken out of my hands. I needed only a few seconds more to react to the change in circumstance.

'Crawford!' I yelled out, ran through the door.

The bracing cold of the night chilled my rushing blood as I darted into the driveway. It was dark, my eyes not fully adjusted as I raised my arms to fend off an incoming blow I'd spotted too late.

I went over, fell flat on my back. It wasn't an easy fall. I wracked my spine and was shot with pain from head to toe. I clenched teeth, tried to roll onto my front to ease the pressure on my spine, and felt a second blow to my side. It was a boot this time. The air evacuated from my lungs as I flung back my head, catching the hard flags. My vision blurred. I couldn't see the figure hanging over me and grabbing my coat front, but I recognised the voice.

'You're finished now, Michie.' It was Gilmour.

Councillor Crawford was beside him, ranting. 'I told you this is what we'd get!' He paced around at my legs, his voice flitting between high drama and flat-out panic. 'You had to balls it all up, didn't you? Wouldn't listen to me, would you?'

My eyesight started to return. I saw Gilmour's face clearly now. He scrunched his features up as he pointed towards his chest with his index finger outstretched. 'Me? You're blaming me,' he changed the direction he pointed, aimed his finger at me, '... for this idiot!'

Crawford took a handful of his own hair. 'You're the one who ...' he seemed to gather himself some, jutted his jaw as he spoke, 'you're the one who *caused* this whole situation.'

'How am I? All I did was what *you* told me.'

'I never told you to kill the girl!'

Gilmour pushed me aside, stepped over me. He didn't seem to realise that I was still holding the gun. 'I didn't do that, don't be putting that on me. I'm warning you, mate, don't even be thinking about that.'

They fronted up to each other. Gilmour pumped out his chest; I saw the Councillor start to retreat, following his earlier, enthusiastic steps in reverse. 'Well, if I don't blame you, tell me ... who do I blame?'

I'd heard as much as I wanted. I knew if I didn't seize the moment, I was finished and Kirsty's killer would go free. I lifted the gun, took aim at Gilmour's back as he spoke. 'We're all in this together. You told me to take care of it and I did … How was I to know she had a problem with fits? All I did was noise the girl up a little, put a bit of a fright on her … Shut her up, that's what you said!'

I pulled the trigger for a second time. The hammer fell as before, but the thud now produced a blue flash accompanied by a loud bang. I felt the gun drop from my shaking hand as the recoil kicked. I waited for Gilmour to fall, to drop to his knees, wail perhaps. He stood still, unmoving for a second until Crawford pushed past him and quickly recovered the shooter from his driveway.

'Jesus, you left the gun in his hand!' he said.

Now Gilmour turned round; he snatched the Webley from the Councillor. 'He tried to shoot me.'

I watched Gilmour wave the gun around. He pushed it into Crawford's chest, then his stomach. 'He had this pointed at me.'

I felt my stomach press against my aching backbone; my legs stiffened. I tried to shove myself away, find the energy to make an attempt at escape but I was lacking coordination. My brain was still reeling from the earlier blow; my back and sides screamed in dual agonies of muscular spasm as I tried to move.

Crawford shouted, 'Get him off my drive.' He swept away the gun in Gilmour's hand. 'And get that out of here … Christ Almighty, a gun just went off in my driveway!' He raised himself on his toes, looked agitated. 'My neighbours are probably calling the police already.'

'Calm down,' said Gilmour. 'That's a busy road there. They'll think it was a car backfiring.'

Crawford wasn't buying it. 'Get him out of here! Get him off my property, now!'

Gilmour smiled as he looked at me, squirming on the ground. 'And what do you want me to do with him?'

'I don't care.' Crawford's voice was pitched higher than

falsetto. His performance, accompanied by flailing arms, was operatic. 'Get him away from here. Get him out of my sight!' He grabbed Gilmour's hand, the one with the gun. 'And take that with you.'

I felt a familiar taste. At some stage in the proceedings I'd bit my cheek. Blood lined the insides of my mouth. I twisted my head enough to spit on the ground. 'You won't get away with it,' I muttered as Gilmour approached. I knew my voice sounded weak, pathetic. At once I wished I'd saved my spit to send in his direction instead.

He leaned over, grabbed my lapels. 'I already have, Michie. Don't you get that?' He drew back the gun, his face firmed as he swung hard. I felt the iron connect with my head and then everything swam.

Chapter 32

I didn't know where I was but it was dark and dank-smelling. I could hear water, perhaps the river, or the sea; it was a substantial body of water. My mouth was bleeding and in greater volume than before. I'd lost some teeth, could feel the gaps with my tongue. One seemed to have snapped off at the root. The pain was intense. The only thing that mitigated it were the agonies of my skull which felt like it had been cleaved open with a claymore. I'd had doings in the past – proper goings over, some of them recently – but this felt serious: like I'd been dropped from an aircraft.

I made an effort to move my hands and that's when I felt the shackles. I was too disorientated to understand quite how I'd been tied but then a match was struck and a storm lantern brought a dim glow to the proceedings.

'I was wondering when you'd come round.'

Gilmour.

My eyes were still smarting, still struggling with the light, but the voice was unmistakeable.

I spat some blood on the ground, rattled the chains that held me to the wall. 'What are you playing at?'

He walked towards me, holding out the lantern. I saw he had a cigarette burning in his fingers; my lungs screamed for nicotine. 'You're in no position to be asking questions, mate.'

'You're right … and you needed to tie me up to even the odds, I suppose.'

'Nice try, Michie.' He drew deep on the cig, knuckles bruised and bloodied. He watched me follow the action and must have sensed my craving as he leaned over and clamped the filter in my mouth. 'Here, I think it's tradition or something … the condemned man and all that.'

I drew deep on the cigarette. One of the fake Regals. 'This your brand, is it?'

Gilmour refused to bite, his face unmoving. 'Seen the price of fags these days? Utter robbery, so it is.'

I tutted. 'You seriously think you're providing a service, a legitimate alternative. What about the boatloads of drugs, or the girls you shipped over to work as sex slaves … that all grist for the mill, is it, Gilmour?'

His lip curled a little; his eyes lit. 'Don't be playing the high and mighty with me, Michie … see those lumps on your head? They were payback for more than a few you dealt me in my day.'

The cigarette had burned to the filter. I spat it onto the wet floor. A low fizzing noise came as the burning tip was extinguished in the water. A shiver passed through my painful shoulders.

'You got what you deserved,' I said. 'Going by the way you turned out, I regret we never laid into you a bit harder.'

Gilmour drew back a fist. He had it aimed at my face but suddenly lowered his arm and grabbed my jaw instead. He leaned into my face as he spoke. 'I never killed that lassie … she just carked it on me. What was I supposed to do?'

I jerked my face from his hand. 'Even if that was true, *even if* …' I paused, made sure I had his full attention, 'how could you let your own son take the blame?'

Gilmour backed up; the lantern in his hand swayed slightly as he turned from me. He resented being called to book, but wanted the last word. 'I never knew he was my son ...'

'Don't give me that. The girl, Kirsty Donald, she knew. She recognised you and that's where the problems started. You went round to put a scare on her, frighten her into shutting up and leaving you and your cronies alone. But she clocked you. She knew you were Glenn's father!'

Gilmour turned round. The lantern's flame jumped; shadows danced on the wet walls. 'Don't twist it,' he said. His voice rose. 'I'd only just found out he was my boy ... Lyn never told me. She told him and that's how I found out. I never knew him like a son. He was just some lad that showed up one day.'

'And that makes it okay, does it?'

'Aye, it does to me!' Pools of water splashed beneath his boots as he paced. 'I mean, so what if he's blood? Life's hard. I don't remember anyone from my family helping me out, doing me any favours.'

I could see I wasn't going to get anywhere playing the moralistic card. Gilmour was an animal; he was out for himself and that was an end to it. He'd as good as killed Kirsty Donald and he didn't care who took the blame – even his own son – so long as it kept him off the hook. He was a criminal, had been his whole life. He'd progressed from shopliftings and slashings, and eventually wound up in a big house with connections in all the right places. He didn't care what he had to do to maintain that, to protect himself.

'You won't get away with it, Gilmour.'

He was lighting another cigarette from the lantern. 'Oh aye, that right, is it?'

I spat some more blood out. 'They're onto you. Kirsty made complaints, in writing ... I got the files.'

He drew on the filter-tip. 'So what? I can deal with that.'

'You think Crawford, or your mates in the Craft can

help you out?' I shook my head vehemently, 'Not a chance. Crawford's finished. He'll sell you out and you know it. And the Craft only look after their own when it suits them. They won't let this mess put a stain on their organisation, trust me.'

Gilmour looked at his watch. 'You finished?'

I shrugged. The movement sent a spike of pain through my shoulder blades.

'I hope you're finished, Michie, because I am. Well and truly finished.'

'Adding me to the list won't make an ounce of difference. You're the one who's finished. I know it, and you know it.'

His facial muscles relaxed as he walked towards me and took two sharp pulls on his cigarette. He thinned his gaze, took a long stare in my direction with the lantern raised and then passed the remains of his cig into my mouth. 'No more words, Michie. This really is the end.'

I'd never wanted a cigarette to last so long. As I scanned the confines of what was going to become my final resting place, my mind latched onto old preoccupations. I didn't want to think of joining my mother, and my father, in any afterlife. What I was looking forward to was a release from all life. This one had been hard enough. The thought of no more struggles, of complete freedom, appealed to me. But, somewhere inside me, I had a desire to go on.

I thought of Lyn, of that day when I drove back to Auld Ayr Toun. She looked so lost, so confused. She was a woman bereft of any reason to go on. She'd lost the one thing that had kept her going through the blackness of her vertical fall. I'd vowed to help her, to help Glenn and I knew I had failed. This fact, perhaps more than any other, stayed with me now. It burned in me, a small fire, a dim glow but it was there. Lyn needed me, more than anyone had ever needed me. Was that my reason for going on? Was that why I had helped her? Had I sensed the need, and inwardly – unconsciously – seized it as a reason for me to keep putting on my shoes in the morning.

I rolled the cigarette's filter along my tongue. Some blood had stuck to the paper; it was thick, gelatinous. I knew I'd been holding the cigarette too long. One more draw and I'd take burning embers of the foul tobacco into my mouth. I pinched my lips and spat the cig into the wet ground.

'What about Lyn, did you not think what this would do to her?'

Gilmour seemed halted by the thought. 'Lyn's nothing to me.' He let a thin smile creep up his face. 'What are you playing at, Michie, sniffing around my cast-offs?'

'She was too good for you.'

He laughed, looked at me and pointed a finger. 'And I thought you were just after a piece of me!' Gilmour started to move his hips, drew an imaginary female form towards his groin and swayed into it. 'Mind you, she was quite the goer back then, our Lyn.'

'Shut the hell up, Gilmour.' My blood surged as I stared at him: laughing and gyrating. I yelled out, 'Christ knows what she saw in you … you're the worst kind of trash.'

He continued to grind his hips, to laugh and wink at me. 'Oh, Michie, I was a bit of rough, don't you know anything? Some women like that, and by God our Lyn liked it rough … As rough as she could get it.'

I turned my gaze away, because anything else was playing into his hands.

Chapter 33

Gilmour wandered around but kept a firm stare on me all the while. He seemed to be enjoying himself, like he'd actually achieved something. As if his having me tied up was akin to basking in the reflection of a trophy. I followed his gaze, let my eyes burn into him, but it had little effect. He was wrapped up in the sense of his own power. It was a dangerous place for a man to be – and even more dangerous for me. I needed to do something to stop him prancing round his kill; I had to puncture his ego if I was to have had any hope of survival.

I lit the fuse and retreated. 'What the hell is this place anyway?

He looked above my head, then rattled the shackles that held my hands – a bolt of pain shot through my injured arm – I winced as he spoke. 'Now there's a question. And I thought you were the man with all the answers, Michie.'

He was toying with me, like a cat with a mouse. I let my eyes flit about the place, try to find some kind of way out. 'Enlighten me … indulge me, even. Or, don't you know where we are? … Just doing what you're told, Gilmour?'

He ran a hand down the solid stone wall; it was dripping wet. When he removed his hand a layer of thick green slime sat on the surface of his palm. He leaned towards me and wiped the mess down the side of my face. 'This is an old smugglers' hold. The town's full of them ... don't you know anything, Michie?'

I tried to pull away from his hand; the smell made my stomach turn. 'Are you off your head? There's not that many of the old holds in the town.' I remembered reading about the old caverns in my schooldays. The place was littered with them and new ones were always cropping up. The chances of me being found were slim, but I had to pretend otherwise. I scanned the damp walls, felt the cold bite in my lungs. 'How long do you think it'll take the police to find me here? You would have been better tying me up at the Auld Brig. The tourists love it there as well, I hear.'

Gilmour closed his eyes for a moment then opened them wide and stared out into the blackness. 'No-one in this town knows the half of it. The whole place is sleepwalking, in a trance they are.' He turned around, put his wide eyes on me, their whites stood out in the darkness of the cavern like burning match-tips. 'I've got close on a million's worth of gear stashed within minutes of the Port.'

I shook my head, turned away from him and tried to act dismissive. 'And you expect me to believe that? You're all talk, mate.'

'What?' He bit. I'd got to him.

'All talk, you always were.' I rattled the shackles above my head. 'Come on then, untie me, show me this million's worth of a stash!'

He smacked his hip and raised a finger towards me. 'Do you think I button up the back ... think I'm going to fall for that kind of thing?'

I turned down the corners of my mouth. 'So there's no stash, then ... eh?'

He approached me, laughing. As he reached my side he put up his hand. It was still wet with the slime from the wall; he gripped my cheeks. 'I can tell you about my business now, Michie … do you know why?'

I tried to pull my face out of his grip. 'Get off me.'

'I can tell you anything I like because I know you'll never get out of here.' He pushed my head against the wall and retreated. 'At least, not in any kind of state to talk about it.'

He started to laugh as I lunged forward, rattling the chains.

'I don't believe you,' I said.

'Oh, believe it,' he laughed on. 'You're through, Michie. Take a good look around because this is the last you'll see of this life.'

I spat at him. He stepped away, mocked me, clearly out of reach.

'Now, now … temper.'

I spat again and it disappeared into the blackness. 'Well if you've got this stash … why can't I see any of it in here?'

He walked in front of me and held up the storm lantern. His eyes thinned now; his face took on a ghostly yellow sheen. 'You couldn't store anything in here.'

'Why? … Why not? Because you have nothing …'

He lowered the lantern and the intensity of his eyes shone again, 'Well, for a start … this one floods!'

The thought put an icy needle in my heart. 'Floods?'

'Every high-tide. The water comes right up to the top.' He raised the lantern, tapped on the roof of the cavern, to emphasise his point.

My pulse raced. The anger in me started to subside and was replaced with something close to fear. It wasn't a fear for my own life but for the fact that Gilmour might get away with my murder on top of everything else.

He turned over his wrist, looked at his watch. I knew he was milking it, watching my fear and savouring it. 'I'm afraid I'll have to be getting along, mate.' He smiled as he looked up. 'High-tide coming.'

I felt my breath shorten. 'Think about what you're doing,' I said. 'You say you didn't kill the girl, then what's this?'

Gilmour let out a low laugh. 'It's payback, Michie. Plain and simple.' He was smiling as he turned from me.

'Gilmour!'

His footfalls echoed with small splashes as he walked away from me, the light from the lantern dimming every step of the way. I struggled with the shackles, pulled as hard as I could. I felt the pain in my injured arm bite once again but I pushed it aside.

'Gilmour!' I called louder now. I felt the veins on the sides of my head might pop as I struggled in the waning light. 'Gilmour!'

As the hold fell into darkness I heard the sound of a latch being loosened, then a hinge creaking. The next noise I heard was a trapdoor closing, and then the sound of soil being heaped from a shovel stretched into near silence. Soon, the only sound I could make out was the hard pumping of my heart upon my ribcage.

Claustrophobia came to me as the strangest sensation. Suddenly and completely. I felt buried alive, starved of oxygen, suffocating. I knew I was letting my imagination run riot but I couldn't do a thing about it. I was trapped and the outside world seemed as remote as another galaxy.

I tugged again and again at the shackles on my wrists. I tried to pull them from the wall but they were solid, secure. My wrists started to ache, and then the bare one bled. I struggled on, but it was futile.

The water dripping on the walls now felt uncomfortable on my back. I imagined black trails engulfing me, but it didn't happen. An hour passed and nothing happened. I called out, roared. My throat grew sore, my voice hoarse.

I developed a pattern: I called out, then waited for a reply. Not even an echo came. The only sound was the dripping of water in the low pools and puddles of the ground and the scurrying rats. They stayed away at first but soon they came to sniff around my boots.

I swore. I kicked out at them and they retreated but they always came back.

'Away ... go!' No matter how hard I shouted the rats returned, likely drawn by the blood from my wrist.

When all that came was the rats, and no tide waters, I started to think Gilmour had fooled me, that the high-tide was all a scare and that I would be slowly devoured by more and more rats and then as quickly as they appeared they were gone.

'What do they know that I don't?' I said to the walls of the hold.

In a few moments, I got my answer.

As if a tap had been turned, water flowed into the hold. By the bucketful.

Oh, Jesus Christ.

The soles of my feet were quickly covered.

'No. Please ... Tell me this isn't happening.' Nothing seemed real now. Holy mother of God.

Someone had once called me on my religious beliefs. My old friend Tommy had been devout as it suited him and told me that when the odds were against you, when all else seemed lost, everyone prayed. I'd doubted him, but now I experienced the truth of those words.

'Oh God above ...'

As the water lapped at my heels, I prayed. As it reached my knees, swallowed my thighs and encircled my waist in its freezing-cold grasp, I prayed. When the water passed my stomach I called out to the patron of lost causes, Saint Jude, and begged for his help. But no-one heard my pleas. No-one answered my prayers. No-one came.

As the water reached my chest, started to exert an intense pressure on my ribs I started to lose the will to fight.

I felt beyond cold. Beyond freezing. Every bone, every fibre of my being cried out in agony. I grew drowsy, fell in and out of brief spells of catalepsy. My ties to the world seemed to be shifting. I lost all sense of self; imagined I was floating out to sea, towards the sun.

The water was calm there, as warm as a bath. Now, even as I shivered, I felt a warm glow. I seemed to leave my mortal body, and float further out to sea. I was heading towards the sunset.

Friends were calling me, old friends.

Voices I knew, voices I loved.

'Doug ...'

I couldn't answer. I was paralysed in a dreamworld.

'Doug ...'

They kept calling.

'Doug, are you there?'

Chapter 34 – Epilogue

They re-named me Lazarus in the hospital ward. The doctors said they had never seen anyone with lower vital signs when they brought me in. It was a miracle I was alive, apparently. I thought they were laying on the religious significance a bit thick. I'd told no-one about the prayers, I was just glad to be alive.

I had both my arms in bandages now. I had a wrapper like Rab C's on my head, and a couple of drips that went everywhere with me; even the bathroom. I felt weak, drained, but like I said, glad to be feeling anything at all.

The nursing staff were playing up to me; I'd become a bit of a local celebrity since The Post printed my story. I liked to read the opener at least a dozen times a day:

AN AYRSHIRE man is recovering in hospital after a dramatic rescue from a long-forgotten smugglers' hold that also unlocked a murder investigation and prompted a probe into Council, Port and Police authorities.

When I say I read the opener, the rest of the article usually followed. I liked to be reminded that Gilmour was in custody and facing charges for the murder of Kirsty Donald, and my own attempted murder. Likewise, it was

163

good to see the pictures of Councillor Crawford with his coat pulled over his face as he was led away for questioning. The great and good of the Auld Toun had a full-scale gutting coming their way, and I couldn't wait to raise a glass to that.

I folded the newspaper down its centre, turned the pages over once again – the creases were well-established now – and slotted in snugly to the bedside cabinet beside my bottle of Lucozade and the old Alistair MacLean novel I'd liberated from the common area. As I eased my broken body back towards the soft white pillows, and tight, crisp linen that kept me in bed I felt my heart kick with the sight of a familiar face.

Lyn stood at the end of my bed. As I stared at her my thoughts alighted on what Crawford had called her. He'd said she was a slut, a slag. I didn't want to ever think of Lyn that way, but I knew Crawford had sown the seed of doubt in me and I still hated him for that. Almost as much as I hated Gilmour for completing her character assassination in the cavern.

She spoke, softly: 'Hello, Doug …' As I drew my focus away I realised there was someone with her. A tall, rangy youth I hadn't recognised. 'This is Glenn.'

The boy took his mother's introduction as a cue to become animated. He stepped forward and held out a hand. 'I wanted to say, y'know, thanks.'

I looked at the boy. His hair sat in tufts on his head. His eyes were wide and welcoming. He wore a Superdry T-shirt under a checked shirt. I didn't know what I had expected but Glenn looked just like every other young lad I passed on the street; it made me smile, even though I knew he was Jonny Gilmour's son.

'I'd shake your hand, but …' I lifted my bandaged and stookied arms in a pathetic pantomime gesture.

'No worries.' He looked at his mother and nodded,

then sidled towards the open door as if he'd practiced the exit several times over. His appearance was for her sake; at least he thought enough of his mother to do that. Perhaps he was more her son than Gilmour's after all but it didn't matter. Lyn had a son with Gilmour that she'd kept quiet about and that's what troubled me. I knew I could never look at her in the same way – or Glenn either – without judging. Maybe it was all in the past, a minor transgression, but I knew I'd jump on it the very second that our first flush of romance left us. Gilmour would forever inhabit our space – the cause of every drop of spilled milk we cried over.

I spoke first, when we were alone. 'Glenn looks none the worse for wear.'

Lyn gripped her tongue in her teeth, nodded.

'I'm glad he's well, Lyn.'

'Me too.' Her voice cracked. I knew she was taking in the state of me. She'd been hurt too, but in other ways. None of us had got out of this without adding more scars to ourselves.

'Oh, it's worse than it looks,' I said.

'I'm sure it's not.' I thought I saw her wipe a tear from her eye but she masked the movement with a deep breath and a change of subject. She was being brave; I dreaded to think of what she had put herself through before setting foot in the hospital. 'I need to thank you as well.'

I shrugged, tried to play things down. I hadn't got involved to collect any laurels and who's to say my motives weren't every bit as underhand as hers. 'We landed the right result, that's what matters. I'm happy you and Glenn are back together and there's no real damage done.'

Lyn let the strap of her bag fall from her shoulder and lowered herself onto the bed. The already tight blankets tightened further around my bruised legs. 'I can't pretend I feel right about this, Doug … after all that's happened.'

I didn't understand. She seemed to be going off at a tangent. Her face changed shape as I eyed her. I knew what I wanted to do, to hold her, but my injuries precluded that. The little voice in my head that controlled my emotions returned, for the first time in a long time, and told me how much it approved of my air of distance.

'I don't follow,' I said.

She looked at her hands, removed a small peach-coloured tissue from her sleeve and dabbed at her moist eyes. 'I never meant for this to happen. I never wanted this, any of it …'

I still didn't know what she meant, exactly. She could have been referring to any number of preoccupations I held in my mind lately. I knew now most of my hopes had been misplaced; there was no future for us. I saw that there never had been; I'd deluded myself.

I saw it was difficult for Lyn to express what she wanted to say and at the same time I wanted to roar at her, to call her on Gilmour, but none of it mattered now. She was hurting, and she had taken more than her fair share of that already. 'It doesn't matter now, Lyn,' I said.

She turned, stared at me. Her eyes were reddened, tear-lined. 'You're a good man, Doug. But it wouldn't work, not now.'

All my aches and pains relocated to one point, somewhere just shy of the centre of my chest. I still felt something for Lyn, but I knew she was right. She deserved better than the hurt I would undoubtedly bring her now. I smiled and played dumb. 'What wouldn't work?'

I was giving her a 'get out of jail free' card and she knew it, seemed grateful. The tissue went back in her sleeve. 'I'm leaving town.'

I couldn't maintain the same smile, but tried to ease her suffering. 'You need to do what's best for you and Glenn …

you've both been through a hellish ordeal.'

Her lips trembled again; she sucked them in and rose. Her cheeks were flushed, her movements jerky, as she walked towards me. She didn't seem to know what to say, or do, next. She touched my hand with two cold fingers which dwelled for a second or two just south of my knuckles and then were jerked away.

I didn't watch Lyn walk out of my life; I stared out of the window instead.